Praise for *Litany of*

T0013748

"In this engrossing collection, charac[...] tween Costa Rica and the US, attracted and repelled by both coun- tries. They see the flaws and aspirations of each, and Diana Rojas tips the balance in surprising ways. Who will protect us—our fam- ily, saints, government—or are they our downfall? Compassionate and achingly realistic."

—Mary Kay Zuravleff, author of *American Ending*

"If our secrets make us sinners, can keeping another's make us a saint? Like the blue morpho butterfly, whose iridescence is a trick of light that simultaneously shows and conceals its truth, the char- acters in this triptych of tales mesmerize and surprise. They are unforgettable, as are their stories, which in the end is their salva- tion . . . and ours."

—Laura Scalzo, author of *American Arcadia*

"In Diana Rojas' outstanding debut, tradition and the challenges of belonging are the background to a deep and compassionate exploration of migration and change. The families in these stories deal with cultural, social and political environments they no longer know. Sometimes the main characters resist, but in all cases, they have to learn the rules of engagement of two countries in con- stant evolution: the United States and Costa Rica."

—Uriel Quesada, author of *Los territorios ausentes*

"*Litany of Saints* is a richly imagined debut collection. With shim- mering intelligence and emotional veracity, Diana Rojas tells sto- ries about people who left Costa Rica for the United States and ones who returned home. Her characters yearn to escape the cages that entrap them, some of them created by their own mak- ing and others by an ever-shifting set of social, familial and politi- cal circumstances. Rojas is a natural storyteller, and the specificity of these tales poses universal questions about what it means to be a Costa Rican, an American, an immigrant and a human being."

—Michelle Brafman, author of *Swimming with Ghosts* and *Washing the Dead*

"Inventive and engaging, *Litany of Saints* is a colorful exploration of identity from the shifting, chameleonic perspectives of Costa Ricans both at home and abroad. Diana Rojas paints an unflinching portrait of gender, duality, personal agency and the explosion that happens when cultural conservatism crashes against a changing world."

—John Manuel Arias, author of *Where There Was Fire*

# LITANY OF
# SAINTS
• • • • • • • • • • • • • A TRIPTYCH

By Diana Rojas

Arte Público Press
Houston, Texas

*Litany of Saints* is made possible through a grant from the National Endowment for the Arts and the Alice Kleberg Reynolds Foundation. We are grateful for their support.

Recovering the past, creating the future

Arte Público Press
University of Houston
4902 Gulf Fwy, Bldg 19, Rm 100
Houston, Texas 77204-2004

Cover art by Dani M. Jiménez
Cover design by Ryan Hoston

Names: Rojas, Diana, author. | Rojas, Diana. Lives of saints. | Rojas, Diana. Tres Marías. | Rojas, Diana. Familia.
Title: Litany of saints : a triptych / by Diana Rojas.
Description: Houston, Texas : Arte Público Press, 2024. | Summary: "In the opening piece, "The Lives of Saints," an immigrant family from Costa Rica regularly prays to a litany of saints to help deal with all that life throws their way-including alcoholism, marital discord, illness and death-all while adjusting to their new circumstances as "Americans." The narrator, a woman trapped in a subservient role supporting her husband, suffers in silence as the men completely disregard her in life-changing decisions. Recounting her family's attempts to balance a traditional, more conservative culture with the new and exciting one in their adopted homeland, she is forced to reconsider gender roles, assimilation and religion. Costa Ricans, or Ticos, living in the United States return to their native country in two of the three novellas in this thought-provoking collection. They discover it's not the "Switzerland of Central America," the perfect country with good healthcare, education and no standing army. In "Las Tres Marías," three sisters raised in the comparative freedom of Massachusetts who return to live in their parents' home country are barely teenagers when they're labeled gringas and "doomed to become sluts." In "La Familia," Juan Manuel has made a life for himself in Chicago, but when his mother calls him home because his brother has been arrested as a terrorist, he faces an uncomfortable reckoning with his country's involvement in regional violence as the Cold War spreads to Latin America. Revealing the cultural dissonance experienced by immigrants, Diana Rojas' characters grapple with their self-perception as they consider what they're supposed to be and who they want to be. Issues of individualism versus community, loyalty to a distant homeland and a divided sense of identity pepper this intriguing debut"-- Provided by publisher.
Identifiers: LCCN 2023057846 (print) | LCCN 2023057847 (ebook)
ISBN 9781558859944 (trade paperback)
ISBN 9781518508059 (epub)
ISBN 9781518508066 (kindle edition) | ISBN 9781518508073 (pdf)
Subjects: LCSH: Immigrants—Fiction. | Costa Ricans—United States—Fiction. | Costa Ricans—Fiction. | LCGFT: Novellas. | Linked stories.
Classification: LCC PS3618.O5354 L58 2024 (print) | LCC PS3618.O5354 (ebook) | DDC 813/.6--dc23/eng/20231220
LC record available at https://lccn.loc.gov/2023057846
LC ebook record available at https://lccn.loc.gov/2023057847

24 25 26          3 2 1

*To my mother, Clara Rodríguez Rojas, who filled my ears with stories.*

*To my father, Fernando Rojas, who wanted me to tell them.*

# CONTENT

# THE LIVES OF SAINTS

Felipe always said the green wool sweater made me look like an old lady. It wasn't nearly cool enough for it, but I wrapped it around my shoulders out of spite and sat down next to the open window to watch the last of the fireflies frolicking in the end-of-summer breeze. I wondered if it would hurt a lot if I let myself roll out two stories down to the flagstones below. That would be one way to end it. At that moment, it seemed like the most peaceful way out of my decades-old marriage.

It had been pouring when we met my daughter Amalia and her kids at the Denny's on the interstate. We were supposed to have picnicked at the lighthouse beach, but the summer storm rolled in changing our plans. It had been Amalia's suggestion, one of her "Wouldn't it be great?" ideas that she'd get overly enthused about.

"Just like when we were little," Amalia had said. "And my kids can see where you and Dad would take us to play at the beach."

I wasn't going to ruin her wistful recollection by reminding her that the water there had been so polluted that I never let them even put their toes in when they were little. Or that we hadn't really gone all that often since Felipe preferred the

1

coastal beaches to the harbor. Nor had she seemed to realize that when they were teenagers and I'd insist on walking with them over to the lighthouse on an occasional Saturday afternoon, it was usually to get away from one of Felipe's benders. I just went along with her sentimental get-together.

Felipe had been morose that whole day. He'd scowl whenever I tried to strike up a conversation. It wasn't because of the rainstorm. The downpour didn't start until we had pulled out of the driveway to meet Amalia. At the beach parking lot, he pulled alongside Amalia's car, the kids in the back all smiles and waves.

"Don't worry, let's just take this party to Denny's," she said. "The kids love that place! All day breakfasts! It'll be almost as good as the beach to them."

She didn't notice that her father was barely listening.

"You remember where it is, right?"

Felipe didn't respond. Just nodded in her direction.

At Denny's, he perked up a bit as soon as Amalia and the kids sat down.

It didn't take her long to notice Felipe's mood. "What's doing, Dad? Why so sad?"

She talked and arranged the toddler in his seat and doled out the giant menus to the other two, all without taking her eyes off Felipe. "We're not bothered by the rain. Don't worry."

He smiled a sad smile.

"Did you hear about the governor? The Jersey guy?" he asked, with a humorless chuckle.

"Oh, jeeeezus!" she laughed. "What a jerk. It takes him this long to figure out he's gay, and then he asks his beleaguered bride to stand by his side while he announces her humiliation to the world. Did you see her face? What a dope she was! I'd have said, 'No way, dickhead, you're on your own here.'"

His voice was gentle. "Well, Amalia, you know, those of us like the governor know how hard it was to do. Most of us would never do it."

Amalia heard him. I know she did. Her sharp eyes focused for a split second on him, then moved over to me. She only glanced, but she read my anguish. She changed the subject, moved on to something about the baby. But she was knocked off kilter for the rest of the lunch. Her conversation became stilted. I knew she couldn't wait to get out of there.

"Those of us!" Those of us? Felipe was a merciless flirt with waitresses. He'd had affairs on business trips, bringing home shirts smelling of perfume. This was classic Felipe, seeking attention in the most outrageous ways. But this new revelation was the most absurd: pretending to come out to his daughter at a Denny's. Who was the dope now, Amalia?

For some time now I had become the beleaguered bride standing two steps behind with a frozen smile on my face. Felipe wasn't gay, I wanted to say to her. Her father was a jerk who in the past several years had taken up the sport of finding new and more shocking ways to embarrass me, as if daring me to leave. Like telling me he'd be leaving me as soon as the kids grew up . . . over our romantic anniversary dinner, no less. Or badgering the maid of honor at a friend's wedding on the dance floor so much that she looked to the bridegroom to save her from the pervy neighbor. Or letting his twenty-something lover call me to challenge me about who loved him more. She had claimed he was sitting right there next to her. I didn't demand to speak to him.

I had never taken him up on his dares. I had never left. I was his wife. And now, he was supposedly gay, in the closet

3

all these years. I didn't believe it for a second, and I knew I wouldn't muster the courage to walk out the door either.

My marriage had become an embarrassment in my middle age. Amalia might have understood, but she'd never mention it. She'd wish to spare me the shame. Her brothers, Eddie and Henry, played oblivious. The rest of the greater family would chalk it up to his drinking.

I found myself on the window seat that night, battling the desire to roll out, knowing I never would. I had become a cautionary tale: Ruth thought she could change Felipe, but she should have known that in marriage, what you see is what you get.

I think I got duped.

∾∾∾

A few days after the rained-out beach picnic, Felipe was in high spirits for the gathering at Joaquín's. Álvaro, my sister Lucía's oldest, was in from Costa Rica, and it was a typical family get-together to fête the visitor. Amalia and her kids rolled in last. By the time they arrived, Felipe was already drunk, lips stained purple by the wine. I saw Henry and Eddie greet her with raised eyebrows and a nod of the head in their father's direction, warning her. Amalia kept her distance from him; maybe it was his drunkenness. Or maybe she just didn't know how to segue from Denny's.

Felipe kept drinking. He laughed louder and louder. Earlier in the day, when the sun was high, he was, as usual, the life of the party. Even I enjoyed his company at times like that. He'd remembered so many jokes. His wit was so quick, turning common conversations into laughable feasts. The laughter in the yard competed with the jollity of the music

4

from the speakers, but by then, Felipe was becoming a drunken bore.

"Felipe, I don't feel well. Can we go now?" I lied because I knew my embarrassment would mount as the sun set. Felipe was so sloshed that he didn't actually put up a fight. Henry, Amalia and Eddie nervously followed us to the front yard to see us to our car. I knew why.

"Dad," said Henry, flexing his maleness, "Mom's going to drive."

This had been an ongoing battle. Felipe was the best drunk driver I had ever been in a car with, but as soon as the kids had become teenagers, they started battling him about taking the wheel after boozing. I'd play the meek wife because I loathed the recriminations after having forced myself to be the driver. But when they were watching, I was helpless to resist. They wouldn't let me.

Felipe rebuffed Henry, the keys dangling loosely from his hand.

Henry snatched them and gave them to me, a little too forcibly, I thought. Then he moved his father to the other side of the car, where he opened the door and shoved him in. Felipe swatted Henry's hands away from helping him with the seat belt. Amalia and Eddie, meanwhile, stood with their arms crossed, blocking me like football guards, ready to block Felipe should he lunge for me or the keys.

I slipped into the driver's seat and noticed that Joaquín and my younger brother, Tony, were watching from the side gate, pretending they were engaged in a conversation. I smiled, as if nothing was amiss, and waved at them. Our children walked toward their uncles as I pulled out. Felipe's eyes were already half-cast, and I figured he'd be asleep by the time we drove off that street.

5

I was wrong. Once we were out of sight of Joaquín's house, he started in. I can't even remember his complaints. But I still remember the smell of wine in his spittle as it landed on my cheek. We had an hour's ride ahead of us. By the time we merged onto the interstate, only five miles in, his voice was thundering. He was banging on the dashboard, demanding I pull over and let him drive.

"YOU HAVE HUMILIATED ME IN FRONT OF OUR CHILDREN FOR THE LAST TIME," he roared. "Pull over. Pull over this minute and stop being a bitch. PULL OVER!"

I kept my eyes glued on the highway. I ignored him, as Amalia had advised me to keep us safe. I prayed to Saint Christopher. Saint Christopher, protector against car accidents, *ruega por nosotros*.

Felipe would not be placated by my prayers or my silence.

"PULL OVER, I said," he spat at me.

Then, he did the unthinkable. He opened the passenger door on the highway and was preparing to leap out of the moving car.

"FELIPE!" I screamed. I was in the slow lane and screeched to a halt on the shoulder as he stuck one leg out.

The car had barely stopped at an angle, when both his legs were out. Cars whizzed by, horns blaring.

Felipe stuck his head in the car through the open door. "NOW. GET. OUT." he hissed.

"I won't," I managed to say.

He slammed the door and walked away, the tail of his shirt flapping in the breeze created by the passing cars.

He walked away! On the shoulder of a major interstate highway!

"Come back!" I hollered, craning my face toward the open passenger door.

I was afraid of getting hit from behind, so I straightened out the car as he walked away in the opposite direction. I watched him recede in the rearview mirror as I rummaged through my bag with nervous hands, searching for my cell phone and then fumbling to open it. His gait was steady, he was walking with purpose and seemingly unaware of the danger he was bringing upon himself. He did not turn around to look at me.

I called Amalia. "Your father! He's walking up the highway! Amalia! He's going to get killed! What do I do?"

"Mom," she said, her voice tight, "just drive home. I'll go get Dad."

I heard later that Álvaro had volunteered to go with her to hunt for Felipe on the interstate. They spotted him and pulled over. Álvaro wrestled with him on the shoulder, overpowering him with his youth and sobriety. He shoved him into the back seat and sat there with him on the ride back to our house. Felipe was strapped into the back seat, subdued and slumped in a drunken stupor. Without saying a word to me, Amalia and Álvaro helped Felipe into the house, jumped back into the car and went home.

I cried to myself and for myself in bed that night. I called my sister Lucía and told her what had happened. She was the only one I ever told these things to because her husband had been worse. At least Felipe had never pulled a gun on me or our kids, like her husband had. But Lucía had gotten lucky: he died before his time, if you can call twenty years of a shitty marriage "before his time."

"I'm drowning," I told Lucía. "Every day, he just gets worse. He could have killed us both today! Some days, I just hope he leaves and never comes back. But he always returns. And sometimes, he promises he'll change. I just don't think he loves me anymore. Most days, I'm sure he doesn't even like me."

"Do *you* like him?" she asked me.

"I don't know. I'm tired. I've told him he could go, but he doesn't leave, and it would be so wrong for me to walk out. I am his wife. I can't," I said. "You should hear the things he comes out with some days, Lucía. It's humiliating!"

"Leave him," she said. "Maybe you have to, even if just for a little while, before he kills you both or you strangle him *por pendejo*."

We made plans that night, Lucía and me. She had spare rooms. We'd be roommates, like we were as girls in Costa Rica, before she'd gotten married, before we had moved to the United States.

Henry, Amalia and Eddie would watch over their father, she assured me. "Don't worry," she kept saying.

That night with Lucía delivering me from evil, I knew I'd finally leave him. I was no longer worried. When at last I started falling asleep, I felt as peaceful as if I'd rolled out the window, and it hadn't hurt at all.

Felipe slept it off on the sofa for most of the night. It was in the wee hours when I heard him go into the kitchen. I heard him open the cabinet and take out a glass. I heard the tap go on, then a crash, the glass falling, and another bigger crash, his body falling to the hard tiles.

He had his first seizure that night.

∽∽∽

"May I?"

I heard his voice but didn't react. I didn't even stop writing. But my heart started pounding.

"Pardon, Ruth. May I?"

This time, he said my name, and I couldn't not react. He motioned to the empty seat next to me when I looked up and flashed me his fabulous smile, a genuine toothy grin that extended up to his eyes and said, without words, "This is for you, only you." I'd seen him smile like that at the beautiful Gladys, who could reciprocate without skipping a beat and add a knowing wink that would make him laugh. He also did it to Gretel, who'd not so much pretend not to notice as take it for granted, but rumor was that Gretel and he would hook up on the side, casually.

I had no style or verve or experience. Why was he talking to me? I scrambled mentally and tried to appear casually calm.

"Of course," I managed to say and slid over to make room for him at the table.

I was intensely aware of the attention this had generated. Felipe, the darling of the class, had sat next to me. Who was I to merit such favor? I imagined them asking.

Felipe was oh so cute and never at a loss for words. He acted as if this were the most natural thing. After that day, he and I would chat whenever he'd find his way to the seat next to me, which was often. So often, in fact, that one day, I forgot the rules and we walked out of class together and to the bus stop. We were talking and laughing, when my brother Joaquín walked over from his second job to meet me for the ride home, as was our custom. When he came up to us, I froze.

He barked: "What's this?"

Felipe, as if tone deaf, smiled his smile and held out his hand to Joaquín. "Felipe. Pleasure."

Joaquín mumbled a nicety back and shook his hand.

Joaquín, married and with a child of his own at the time, barely said a word to me on the bus ride home. Right before our stop, he broke the silence: "Ruth, you know what he is. Watch out."

∾ ∾ ∾

This is what it takes to become a saint: First, you have to wait five years after the saintly person dies to make sure all the hullabaloo about them is real. Then, someone asks the local bishop to start investigating. If the bishop thinks there's some merit in the stories about the holiness associated with the person, he sends the case up to the vicar of Jesus Christ himself, the pope. That's when the deep dig starts, and the Congregation for the Cases of Saints looks into whether this person's life was so exemplary that their example inspired prayer in others. Then finally, the miracles. If a person's prayer, interceded by this holy person, was answered, then it's positive proof that the candidate for sainthood is in heaven. A second miracle, and it's pretty much in the bag. The candidate gets a halo.

But it's a rigged game. It can be rushed, too. No need to wait five years if the evidence is so overwhelming. That's when there are many miracles, and many people, who came in contact with the supposed holy person, had their prayers answered. But the most important tool to becoming a saint is having a champion. That person, way before his or her death has held the saintly candidate up as an exemplary human being, all of whose humanly flaws have disappeared. And, that champion has to be a person who has never been shy about telling anybody and everybody about the suspected saint's goodness.

My brother Joaquín was our saint. Mamá was his champion. He'd never have to wait five years, because she put a halo on him before the youngest of us were even born.

My first memory is from when I was four. My mother was dressed in a Carmelite nun habit—brown with a rosary embroidered on its apron—in return for some favor she asked of the Virgen del Carmen. She was also very pregnant, so maybe the habit and supposed payback were a convenient way to fit into something, anything. She was handing my sister Lucía and me over to my grandparents, Don Jesús and Doña Juana, at their house on the banks of the Río Tiribí in San Francisco de Dos Ríos, Costa Rica. We lived on the far edge of their land and relished any opportunity to play uninterrupted on their little farm. Mamá would stay home confined until giving birth to my baby brother, Antonio. Tony.

With Tony, we became four—fifteen years between the oldest and the youngest. First Joaquín and his twin, Jesús, the baby who didn't even make it to six months. Mamá grieved for a decade before having Lucía, me and Tony in the space of five years. But no number of babies could replace the baby my mother had lost. Joaquín became a stand-in for his dead twin, embodying all of the dead baby's potential. He became her obsession. When he was miraculously unhurt after a fall from our grandfather's horse at age two, Mamá became fanatical about him and identified in him every virtue and even some magical powers.

In the official version, Joaquín was the savior of the family. When, as a baby, he survived the scarlet fever that took his twin, Mamá tacked on the dead baby's name to his. She, henceforth, was the only one to always refer to him as Joaquín Jesús. When he was a teenager, Mamá would tell friends who came to her with problems, "Take it to Joaquín Jesús, he'll know what to do." If someone needed divine intervention, she'd say, "I'll tell Joaquín Jesús. He'll pray for you."

Later, it would be Joaquín Jesús who would be credited with having the pluck and ambition to try to drag his family out of the poverty caused by our father's drinking. He was the one to lead his family out of Costa Rica and into the promised land: the US of A. The godly Joaquín Jesús, who not only must have led the soul of his twin out of Limbo and into Heaven, also delivered us all to success. "Joaquín Jesús," my mother would say, "is a saint, thinking never of himself but always of others." Our older brother was the lodestar.

That was the history that had been codified since I was a child. It was the origin story that the family had chosen to believe. None of us thought to challenge it. But even back then when I was young, I think I doubted it. The difference between him and the rest of us was that he had been chosen by Mamá. She had made the rest of us bit players in our own lives. We didn't know we could break out of those roles.

For all of our family's history, we had lived in the inconsequential town of San Francisco de Dos Ríos, on the outskirts of San José. My father's father was always called Don Jesús by everyone, including his wife, because he was locally prominent. Don Jesús gave my parents a house on the edge of his land as a wedding gift. Maybe Don Jesús already knew that his youngest son, my dad, wasn't going to amount to much. The house wasn't much to speak of. It had a wood frame, hard packed dirt floors, except for the living room, which had a polished, poured concrete floor, an extension of the porch. Our lives were not luxurious, to say the least. Before he squandered it all, including our house, Papá had been a man of means. He had grown up in a family with land. Don Jesús owned numerous plots of land all over the neighboring canton of Desamparados and along the banks of the Tiribí River in San Francisco. But Don Jesús also had sired numerous children. The males practically all grew into unambitious, heavy-drinking womanizers, which meant that Don Jesús got to live out his years watching the fruits of his labor and his inheritance dissipate at local bars.

One of my earliest memories was of the time we were in Cartago visiting Joaquín, who was at a boarding school there, the highly esteemed Colegio San Luis Gonzaga, named after the patron saint of students. Don Jesús had paid for him to attend, perhaps because he, too, felt that there was something special about Joaquín, as his daughter-in-law had long insisted. Whatever the reason, it added to Mamá's pride in her son. She would make the two-hour trek to reward him with food and clean clothes. If no one else could watch over us, she'd take her babies with her.

∾ ∾ ∾

"Ruth! When you're done working today, head to the photo shop. They're going to take your picture for your school ID."

Papá surprised me with this, saying it nonchalantly over breakfast a week before the academic year was set to begin. At fifteen, I was working for the same family that had long employed my mother, and her mother before her and my sister Lucía. Together we did everything the family housewives — ladies of leisure — didn't want to do. We cleaned, we cooked, we sewed, we minded their kids. I was drafted to work with my mother right after I had graduated from elementary school. It didn't matter that I had graduated with top honors or that my principal had called my mother in to tell her that she had gotten me a scholarship to the vaunted Colegio Superior de Señoritas so that I could go on to high school free from financial worry. It didn't matter that Tony, my champion, had entreated our father with a whining refrain of "Papá, let her go to high school." My parents said no. "For what? So she can find a boyfriend?"

Papá made his announcement a few days before another lost school year was to begin, two years after I'd finished primary school. He was suddenly feeling generous, and I asked no questions. I heard him tell Mamá that the Liceo San Antonio—well below the status of the Colegio Superior de Señoritas—would accept me at the last minute, thanks to his old bar buddy. I resisted the urge to kiss his feet. I went to work and, after work, hurried to the studio for my photo, making it in the nick of time before they closed. I remember picking leftover bits of thread from my sweater right before the photographer snapped the photo.

"*San Luis Gonzaga, ruega por nosotros*," I said silently just as he snapped and caught the image of my mouth slightly pursed in prayer.

When the photos were ready, I picked them up and handed them to my father.

"Thank you, Papá. Thank you for letting me do this. I won't disappoint you. I'll get good grades and still work after school. I'm so happy," I said.

He stayed quiet. Papá had finally stopped drinking that year. Things, it seemed, were looking up. The day before school was to start, he announced gruffly at dinner that I would not be going, after all.

"But why," I wailed. "Why?"

"Stop crying. Stop making such a big deal out of this," he scolded. "Do you think you're more special than the rest? There is not enough money to buy you a uniform or books."

"I'll make my own uniform! I'll sell my necklace to buy books! I'll work before and after school. Please!" I begged.

I cried. I had offered up the thin gold necklace with the medallion of Mary that I had just gotten that year for my

14

*quinceaños*. It had to be worth something. It was worth my education.

"Mamá, he can't do this!" I complained out loud.

Standing at the stove, Mamá kept her back to me.

Papá said it was final. Tony glowered from the other side of the room.

Two years after that disappointment, when Tony was about to start his second year at the local high school, and having reached our father's height, he persuaded Papá to let me enroll in night school. Tony threatened to drop out of high school if I wasn't allowed to attend. All the local boys were going to high school in that era. So were most of the girls. I was seventeen by then.

This time, Papá raised no objections, provided Lucía and I left the house clean in the early morning before heading to our jobs on the other side of town. My days started at 5 a.m., and I would not get back home until past 9 p.m., bone tired but still with homework to do.

Papa's fears were not unfounded. It was during my first year at night school that I met Felipe. When we started talking, Felipe's schedule was not so different from mine, but with one exception: instead of doing homework, he'd head out dancing and partying with Gladys and Gretel and a crowd whose lives seemed less encumbered than mine. He, the girls and other classmates were my first glimpse at another way to live. I was in awe of their freedom. I was jealous, too. In order to be allowed to go to school, I had to agree to have Joaquín come fetch me every night. Neither he nor Papá were worried about my physical safety because crime was not an issue in those days. Both of them were old-fashioned, and they believed that someone had to be there to protect my virtue, to ensure I didn't get comfortable with boys.

The rules in my family were that you dated the guy you were going to marry. Period. As such, Lucía's tale would be tragically familiar. She hastily married the wrong man. She was not even twenty when she started dating a nice boy from the next town. Isaac was his name. But neither he nor Lucía were convinced of the antiquated notions of a quick courtship and marriage, so they dated secretly. It was all very chaste. But even so, when Joaquín found out about it, he snitched on her. She took a beating that day from Mamá, who called her shameless, and accused her of being loose. Soon after that, still mourning the forced breakup with Isaac, she met the suave snake, Douglas, at a family wedding. He charmed his way through Papá and Joaquín by coming to visit daily with groceries in hand. Lucía and Douglas were married early the next year. Before their first week of marriage, it had ended. Douglas had already hocked both of their rings to pay off a debt.

～～～

They suspected astrocytoma. Its most common symptom is a seizure. That indicates that the tumor has been growing undetected in the brain for years until one day, suddenly, it grows a micrometer and presses on a nerve. Other symptoms include behavior and personality changes. I wasn't thinking of that when I found Felipe writhing on the kitchen floor. I figured he had outdone himself drinking that night.

At first, like me, the hospital staff was sure Felipe was just pickled. They thought he'd had too much booze for too long, not just that night. They suspected delirium tremens. I was less sympathetic than pissed. But I sort of knew it wasn't the drink. I hailed from a long line of drinkers and never knew any of them to have delirium tremens. Felipe wasn't even a binge drinker, just your run of the mill alcoholic, a highly functioning one, at that.

I had not thought to tell the doctors about the incident on the highway nor the revelation at Denny's. Or the way he now seemed to get drunker faster and harder. It didn't occur to me that they could be symptoms. They were character flaws.

I knew what Felipe was. By the time I had met my future husband, he was an unfettered grown-up street urchin, the product of an uninterested mother and an unknown father. His older brother, Saúl, had raised him. They were both wickedly smart and able to charm the pants off everyone. Felipe was the handsome one, as well as the more ambitious of the two.

Not two years after Felipe and I had developed our relationship, he took off to Las Vegas, Nevada, seeking adventure and a new life. Neither Joaquín nor Papá knew about us. Felipe promised to write, and he did, faithfully, every week, sending the letters undetected to the P. O. Box we had and that I was responsible for. He had landed in the United States knowing just one friend, who had preceded him by three months in Las Vegas. His friend helped him get a job as a dishwasher at the Riviera Hotel and Casino. Within months, Felipe had learned English, and his million-megawatt smile had assisted him in getting to the front of the house as a busboy. He then flirted his way around tables, where the ladies would tip him generously.

∞ ∞ ∞

A few months after Felipe had left for Las Vegas, Joaquín announced that he had been offered a job in New York City. He had at that time been working at one of the few fancy restaurants in San José, and an American tourist had so appreciated the attention he had received from Joaquín that he offered him a job at the hotel he managed. Very attracted to Joaquín, the tourist assured Joaquín that his Latin looks would get him far in the New York City restaurant scene. It was an offer he couldn't refuse. The tourist assured him that in one week in New York he could make the same money it took him two months to make in San José. Joaquín got his papers together and boarded a plane for the first time in his life.

Joaquín's wife, María de los Ángeles, and their toddlers were to move into our already cramped house until Joaquín could send for them. Ángeles, as we call her, was misnamed. She was actually, truly, no angel. Her marriage to Joaquín had been more proof to Mamá that her oldest son was blessed and watched over by his twin in heaven. Ángeles was the belle of the town, the beautiful daughter of a prominent family. She was educated. She had never worked. Her sister had gone to the United States in the late 1950s and married a man there, settling in Queens, New York. Their mother, who treated her daughters as *mis reinas,* insisted that Ángeles join her sister in the place that bore their pet name. She believed that Ángeles had long ago outgrown provincial Costa Rica and was too sophisticated for its confines. Behind Angeles' sweet and smiley face, there was a mean and snobbish shrew, who when Joaquín wasn't looking, treated all of us, Mamá and Papá included, with disdain.

"Ruth," she would say, "it's too bad you didn't apply yourself more at school when you were younger. A good education is what allows women, like me, to get ahead in life and marry well." Or, "It's too bad that Tony takes after his father. It might be my imagination, but he tends toward being lazy, right?"

We detested her. Mamá would scold us if we even tried to complain or, God forbid, mimic her behind her back.

"She is your brother's wife. He loves her," she would snap. End of discussion.

The original plan was to put Ángeles and the babies in my room, and me with Tony in his room, which was really just a glorified closet. Ángeles would not stand for it. Her children, she said, were accustomed to better things in life, so we were both kicked out of our rooms and had to set up cots in the living room every night and close them up and store them every morning. The toddlers got a room all their own.

With Joaquín gone, Mamá made sure Ángeles was happy. And to make Ángeles happy, she added just a few more things to my morning chores: cleaning her room, making her bed, washing the babies' clothes and preparing their breakfast, leaving it served on the table and ready for them for when they'd eventually get up.

Ángeles would hold court in our living room, inviting her lady friends over in the afternoon for coffee. She'd sit alone on the upholstered side chair, obsessively smoothing the skirts of her store-bought American dresses, hand-me-downs from her sister, drawing attention to their up-to-date fashion. There, in stage whispers, she'd explain that Joaquín had to leave in order to make more money, since Papá had taken out a mortgage on the house that he couldn't afford to pay back. "The horror!" she'd say dramatically. "They were about to lose their house until he volunteered to pay it back, for his mother's sake, of course."

Mamá's face would not change, but the rest of us burned with shame. It was true that Papá had taken out a mortgage on the house that was his wedding gift, free and clear. But he did it to finance a *pulpería* in town. It was true that he had skipped payments on the debt, but not because he was lazy or drinking—he had stopped by then—but because he was a terrible businessman. Of course, he hadn't bothered to tell Mamá about the failing finances. It was Abuela Juana who stopped in one afternoon and spoke in low tones to her at the stove, telling her that the house was about to be lost, telling her that Don Jesús had refused to bail Papá out, telling her she was so sorry.

But it was a lie that that Joaquín was bailing us all out by himself. All of us were working hard to pay off that debt. In fact, Abuela Juana had barely shut the door, when Mamá rushed up the street to her brother Alejandro's house and asked him for a loan. Alejandro was famously uncharitable. He had some money but believed everyone had to pull themselves up alone. He did, however, have a soft spot for his little sister and agreed to pay the debt, the whole debt, but only after having her sign her X on a scribbled note that said she understood 100% that it was a loan, requiring payback, and not a gift. The house would not be lost.

The day after Mamá had asked her brother for salvation, she sat Lucía, Tony and me down after dinner and laid out the facts. Together, we came up with solutions to make extra money that could go toward paying off the loan. Lucía, still single at that time, and Mamá would take in laundry and ironing and tackle it after dinner. I was tasked with helping Mamá make tamales and *cajetas* to sell at Papá's store on weekends, when the men hung out there downing shots of *guaro* and working up an appetite. Tony had to collect eggs from our chickens and buy some from the neighbors to sell door to door on his way to school.

"Pray to San Sebastián," she said. He was the patron saint of perseverance and courage. *San Sebastián, ruega por nosotros.*

Joaquín had not been at our planning session. At that time, he was at his own house making plans to leave for New York. I don't know if Mamá went over later to tell him what happened. She probably wouldn't have asked him to contribute outright because he was a man and had his own family to fend for. But I'm sure that he would have offered some of his new salary to help. He was that kind of guy.

When I complained to Mamá that Ángeles was slandering us all by not telling the whole story, she shrugged and tried to soothe me: "What difference would it make to call her out? Let her be. She needs to believe what she says."

None of us were teary-eyed when Joaquín sent for Ángeles six months later. They settled into a two-bedroom apartment in Queens, in the same neighborhood as her regal sister. We went about our lives, but it was mere months before Joaquín convinced Papá to also give the United States a try. After all, Joaquín reminded Papá that his *pulpería* wasn't profitable and would never get the family ahead, so he had nothing to lose.

"Joaquín Jesús knows what's best for us," Mamá insisted.

Papá, encouraged by our mother to listen to our older brother, took off for Queens.

It was 1965, and I was nineteen. Lucía was married and very pregnant. When I wrote to Felipe to tell him about Papá's departure, he wrote back immediately, excitedly expressing his hopes that we would all soon follow.

"This is a good country," he wrote. "Nobody cares what you were or who you came from. They only care that you know how to work. You really can become whoever you've dreamed of being here. You get your one chance at reinventing yourself. If you squint a little, this place is utopia."

❧ ❧ ❧

It took more than a week for the doctors to figure out how to control Felipe's seizures. Throughout that time, he was either sleeping (sedated), combative (headed for sedation) or just groggy (coming out of sedation).

I found myself unable to leave his side.

The kids would come in to spell me. They'd try to get me to go to the cafeteria to have lunch or coffee or get fresh air. And they'd offer to sit by their father's side while I went home to shower or sleep in my own bed. Sometimes, I took them up on their offers, but I bounced right back to his side as soon as I had lunch or showered or whatever it was I had left for.

Henry and Eddie would often take turns sitting with me, trying to distract me with idle chatter or Scrabble. Amalia was more of a silent presence. I could feel her watching me when I closed my eyes. Watching Felipe. I felt her judgment.

"You're allowed to be angry, Mom," she finally blurted out one day deep into the week. "You can be furious. He was an ass. And, let's be real, he might have brought this upon himself."

I didn't trust myself to answer her. I let it slide. I said nothing. But all that night, I waited for the anger to bubble up. I tried to feel the righteous indignation I had felt when Lucía and I hatched the plan for my escape. I tried to feel like I wanted to escape. But I was no longer desperate. I'd look at Felipe's sleeping face and remember the early days, the days right after we had gotten married. Or when the kids were little, and we'd pile in the hot car and hit the road in July for our two-week vacations. Or when he'd unwind on weekends by playing record after record after record, banging along on his bongos or sometimes grabbing me to dance.

I tried to remember the jerk. But my brain would only shrug, telling me, "Let it be."

∾ ∾ ∾

Papá sent for us February of 1966. Lucía was devastated. Joaquín made her an offer: Once she gave birth, he'd send for her and the baby on the condition that she leave that good-for-nothing Douglas behind. He knew that guy was a zero from the get-go, he said to her. Lucía refused; she didn't want people to think her baby had no father. We hugged like we'd never see each other again, and I promised I'd send for the three of them as soon as I could.

Mamá, Tony and I landed on a cold, blustery Thursday. They were all there to greet us: Papá, Joaquín, a very pregnant Ángeles and their two young children. Ángeles handed Mamá a gray wool coat and me a gigantic green suede shearling-lined one. It was two sizes too big, but heavenly in its warm embrace. I loved it!

But Mamá, who liked things and us to look perfect, frowned a little and said, "You can move the buttons over to-morrow to make it fit better."

We all moved into Joaquín and Ángeles' apartment: Mamá and Papá in one bedroom; their kids, Tony and I in the second bedroom; and the hosts in the living room on a bed that was set up there every night and taken down each morning. It was a tight squeeze.

By the front door to the apartment, there was a framed photo of St. Frances Xavier Cabrini, the first American citizen beatified as a saint. Mother Cabrini, patroness of immigrants, *ruega por nosotros*.

By Monday, Tony had been enrolled in the local high school, and I was escorted to my first job. One of Ángeles' friends had gotten me a position at a coat factory, sewing buttonholes. Ángeles didn't work; she tended to her children and her current pregnancy. Mamá and I tended to her house.

"Gratitude, Ruth," whispered my mother when I shot her a glance after Ángeles announced that arrangement. "She's the queen of this house."

The factory work was factory work, but not awful. The awful part was passing the bus stop with all the young people on their way to high school. They'd stand out there in the freezing cold, boys and girls laughing and talking, with books in their arms pressed against their bodies to stay warm. None of them noticed me as I passed in my big green suede coat with the buttons moved over. I was only slightly older and probably still could have been their classmate. When Papá sent for us, I imagined that my life would change and that I'd become a carefree American like those kids I now saw at the bus stop.

I didn't become them. I worked with mostly Italian and Greek ladies, all older than me. No one spoke my language, but they were incredibly kind to me. Because we did piece-work, they'd take turns putting pieces on my piles when the supervisor made his rounds, until my fingers became nimble enough to work as fast as the others. Once, one of the Italian ladies sent me home with a letter for Joaquín, asking permission to have me over for tea after work. She promised to put me on the correct bus home afterward. She jabbered all through the tea. I didn't understand a word she said but smiled and nodded and enjoyed the biscotti she offered. It was the only overture of friendship I had received to that point.

Felipe's letters started coming to the house. When Joaquín caught on to them, he scowled and, for the first time I can remember, became cross with Mamá: "How long has this been going on?"

Mamá looked at me, not knowing what to say. Here, like in Costa Rica, I was the one who brought in the mail. She hadn't known about any of the letters.

"Joaquín," I answered in defense of my mother, "Felipe heard from one of our old classmates that we moved here, and he's sent me a letter. He says he's far away, in Las Vegas."

Joaquín calmed down but he still felt the need to note to everyone what a loose guy Felipe was, of questionable parentage, and really just a slouch and a partier.

"Don't be a dope, Ruth," he warned. "You know what he is."

The letters kept coming, as did Joaquín's warnings and disapproval. And, when I announced to the family later that year that Felipe had written to say that he would be moving to Queens, Joaquín was beside himself. But for once, my father didn't seem to feel threatened by the presence of a suitor. Joaquín, however, egged on by Ángeles, was immediately up in arms.

"The nerve on him! I hope he doesn't expect me to help him find a job just because we're compatriots. Some people! They're just users. They really think they can use everyone else to get to the top. Well, he's in a for a big surprise. . . ." and on and on and on.

"I can't imagine what made him decide to move east," needled Ángeles. "Ruth, you're not leading him on, are you?"

That was mid-November. By the first week of December, Felipe was in Queens. He'd taken a cross-country bus and landed on the couch of his brother Saúl's acquaintance. The very next day, a Saturday, he was at our door introducing himself to my parents, shaking Joaquín's hand, meeting Ángeles and Tony, and enchanting the children, who immediately fell in love with him.

That afternoon and into the evening, Felipe regaled us with the wonders of the country he had seen from the window of the bus. He told tales of the characters he met: cowboys in Colorado, farmers in Kansas, the slow, sweet drawls of Kentucky that he struggled to understand, the blues guitarist who serenaded them for a long part of the voyage. Through his eyes, we saw our new country.

They never said it in so many words, but Mamá and Papá fell in love with him, too. He was a breath of fresh air in that stale, overcrowded apartment. Tony fell in love with him too, especially when the two of them started to talk about music and all the great bands they'd discovered in this land of musical treasures.

Felipe, who had never experienced the close-knit affection of a family home, fell in love with us all, but especially with Mamá, who babied him in a way she hadn't babied anyone else, except Joaquín. Felipe would reward her every proffered meal or snack or cup of coffee with a hug and his gorgeous smile, as if it were fit for a king.

Mamá, after that first meeting, encouraged Joaquín Jesús to ask at the hotel restaurant, where he and Papá were working, if there was room for Felipe. Felipe was hired on but lasted less than a month there.

To Joaquín's horror, Felipe came by after one Saturday shift and said, "You know, brother, this is not for me. I bussed tables in Las Vegas, and I know I can do it here. But I want more. I want something else. I want to work with my brain." Felipe tapped his head with his finger as he said this, then held out his hand.

Joaquín was dumbfounded by what he perceived as a lack of gratitude and withheld his handshake. "You're telling me that the job I got you is not good enough for you? That the money that is good enough for me to support my family is not good enough for you? Get out of here!"

Felipe was surprised by the outrage and looked apologetically at Mamá, who shrugged and made a gentle sign with her hands for him to leave and that she'd handle it. He came to me, kissed my cheek goodbye and left.

I wasn't privy to Mamá and Joaquín's conversation, but I did hear something about "Ruth is happy." I was surprised that my mother had noticed that I was indeed happy. In Felipe, not only did I have someone my own age to converse with, but he was also showing me a whole new world, even if only from my living room, where he'd come to court me at least three or four times a week. Because he could talk so animatedly about topics ranging from rock music to politics, history and fashion, he entertained all of us, even Ángeles. We had all looked forward to his visits. Mamá would even open beers for him and place them in his hand, so he wouldn't interrupt his conversations.

Despite Joaquín's disappointment about Felipe leaving the job, he too had grown to enjoy Felipe's company. As a family, then, we were all relieved when Felipe told us a week later that he had landed a job at a men's clothing store in Hoboken. In fact, his leap of faith into the unknown, getting a job across the Hudson and moving to an efficiency there, inspired Mamá and Papá to also find us our own apartment, down the street from Joaquín's.

At the clothing store in Hoboken, Felipe quickly became the salesman regular buyers favored. By June of the following year, Felipe's upward trajectory continued, and he was offered a job in Connecticut. His eye for color and fashion did not go unnoticed, and a friend of a friend had turned him onto the job at the Gant shirt factory in New Haven. His new duties were not on the floor but in the offices, picking cloth and patterns for the shirts destined for wear by the Ivy League crowd.

"I might not be able to go to that great university," he said to me with a wink, "but they'll be carrying me on their backs with these clothes."

With a promising line of work, then, Felipe asked me to marry him.

I stammered. I blushed. "You have to talk to Papá. You have to talk to Joaquín," was all I could say.

"I don't want to marry them. I want to marry you. I want to know if you want to marry me," he said, looking into my eyes.

"Of course," I said, knowing full well that my brother would not likely forget Felipe's defiance of convention.

∾ ∾ ∾

More than a week had elapsed before Joaquín finally came to visit Felipe in the hospital. Felipe had stopped seizing every couple of hours, but the drugs made him practically catatonic. The scans had strongly hinted at astrocytoma, but they wouldn't know for sure until they did a biopsy. But first, Felipe would need to stabilize.

"Ha! So the fast life finally caught up with you," joked Joaquín, patting Felipe hard, manlike on his reclined shoulder.

Felipe barely noticed.

"The doctors don't think it's the drink," I said, tight lipped. "They're thinking cancer. Brain cancer."

Joaquín looked hard at Felipe, pensive. Then he said with forced gaiety, "Ah, this cat always figures a way out! He's got nine lives. Before you know it, he'll be cracking open a six pack and regaling us all with the tale of his hospital vacation."

I knew Joaquín was trying to console me. I smiled.

Felipe seemed to have registered the comment and weakly waved his hand in agreement, a crooked half-smile on his lips.

"I'll take this to Santa Rita," Joaquín promised me. Santa Rita, patron saint of impossible causes, *ruega por nosotros.*

Felipe and I would sit for hours holding hands. When he was awake, he'd look at me as I chattered away, trying to entertain him with mundane tales and gossip. I didn't get the feeling that he was entertained, but I'd go on because he had a worried look in his eyes. I had no answers, so I avoided all questions.

I called Henry the day the doctors wanted to explain their findings to us. Ill at ease, Henry had no idea how to address his father's mortal condition. He kept couching the findings in positivity, "Brain tumor, Dad, but SUUUPER slow growing. It's probably been there for decades! You'll need some rehab, but before you know it, you'll be out running a 10K again. . . . This is just a life test, Dad, throwing obstacles in your way to see how well you can maneuver."

The doctor never said any of those things. Felipe flashed me a glimpse of that look he'd give me when our kids acted dorky or idiotic. I almost busted out laughing from relief. Henry was being a dork, but more importantly, Felipe was coming back.

∾ ∾ ∾

Felipe and I had a small wedding. He was earning $125 a week at the factory offices, and we were convinced that we were rich. I told him I did not want to find work outside the house anymore, and he supported the idea of me becoming a housewife. We bought a car, a new-to-us yellow Plymouth with camel-colored seats. We bought furniture and a stereo. We invited the family over for weekend visits to our little townhouse in New Haven. We didn't care that it was on the sad side of town. It was the one property that hadn't turned us down because we were foreigners. We loved it. We were becoming American. We took road trips, we had friends who were not related to us and I was learning English—Felipe had already learned in Nevada. Felipe thought I didn't know, but he'd smoke dope with the neighbor men out by the communal picnic table in the evenings, their laughter making its way into the house, where we ladies drank wine from wicker-wrapped bottles and talked about nothing important. We worked on our GEDs.

I relished the trappings of success. I can't say I didn't like it when we'd roll up to Joaquín and Ángeles' apartment and Felipe would honk our arrival so that the kids would run to the window and scream, "They're here!" They'd run down to greet us, climbing into the car and onto Felipe's lap, where he'd let them pretend to drive and honk the horn.

Mamá would hug him. Papá would strike up a conversation and sit by him for hours. Tony didn't hide how cool he thought Felipe and I had become. Joaquín was jealous but tried not to show it as he awkwardly steered the conversation to his latest success: becoming head waiter at the hotel restaurant.

Before our second anniversary, I was pregnant with Henry. Rather than congratulate us outright, Joaquín thought it appropriate to joke about the delay. After all, immediate pregnancy after marriage was proof of a virtuous couple and the virility of the husband. "Maybe all the gays in the clothing industry have been rubbing off on Felipe," he said, winking. Felipe glared at him, and Joaquín smiled and raised his glass to Felipe, saying, "Better late than never, *maricas*."

The men in the room, and Ángeles, laughed and responded with, "*¡Salud!*"

"I'm happy for you," Mamá said to us quietly, out of everyone's earshot, when we said our goodbyes at the end of the night. "I'll pray to San Gerardo for you and your baby every night until it arrives."

San Gerardo, patron saint of pregnant women and unborn babies, *ruega por nosotros*.

The next week, Mamá was dead. We were all sitting around her living room after our regular Sunday dinner. She had been feeling poorly all day, so I had done the cooking for her. She had barely eaten, and, at the end of the meal, she had tried to excuse herself to her bedroom. Instead, we guided her to the living room, where the men drank whiskey. Felipe told a joke, and, while we were all laughing, Mamá clutched her chest and stared straight ahead. Before we could react, she fell face-first off the sofa. We all sprung up simultaneously. Someone started yelling instructions, another started banging on her chest and breathing into her mouth.

Felipe stood over her and her would-be saviors hollering, "DON'T GO! COME BACK!"

It was mayhem. We were all running around, calling an ambulance, locking the kids in a bedroom, crying and screaming. Papá looked like he was about to collapse next, slumped onto the sofa she'd fallen out of and watched as if in a catatonic state. San Juan de Dios was called upon. San Juan de Dios, patron saint of heart attacks, *ruega por nosotros*.

By the time the ambulance came, we knew she was gone. But Felipe wouldn't give up. By then, he had knelt by her side, her limp hand in his, and kept howling at her to not leave him. It took Joaquín and Tony, together, to pull him away, so they could wheel her lifeless body out the door.

We were all inconsolable. Felipe was destroyed. For a little more than two years of his life, such a short time, he had a mother, my mother, who had shown him love and had given him a glimpse of what he had missed growing up. He barely spoke for a week.

I don't believe Joaquín approved of Felipe's public display of grief. Perhaps he found it showy. Maybe he thought it fake, like those hired wailers paid to amplify a family's grief. I think he resented Felipe's role as the visible face of the family's loss, resented the mourners at the funeral offering my grieving husband condolences, giving him hugs, trying to dry his tears.

I remembered how Joaquín had grimaced momentarily at me when, overcome with emotion, Felipe couldn't get through the first reading at the funeral Mass, and Tony had to step in and read the first and the second himself. And Joaquín had conveyed his shame for me with raised eyebrows when Felipe couldn't hold his head up while bearing the casket because he was trying to hide his bawling face.

"You'd think it was his own mother who died," he said after food and drinks when we returned from the cemetery. Felipe pretended not to hear. No one shushed him.

"Listen, *chavalito*," he said to Felipe several weeks after the funeral, when I was just starting to show a little, "your Ruth is now motherless in a foreign country. She has no friends but you in that Connecticut you've taken her to. You'd better not fail. Now, it's me watching you, and I'm no softy like my mother was."

My father did not get involved. He let Joaquín become the patriarch, and Ángeles made it known that she had officially been crowned matriarch. We didn't protest. After that first long, sad year, Tony brought home Liliana, a recent arrival from Puerto Rico who became his bride in short time. Ángeles had loads to say about what she perceived was a lack of class on the part of Liliana: she laughed too loudly, her dancing was vulgar, she dressed too provocatively and, worst of all, she was Puerto Rican. As a stand-in for his mother, Ángeles felt the need to counsel Tony not to marry her. I loved Liliana and let Tony know as much. She had grown up in a more open family, where girls could laugh and enjoy life as much as the boys did. She was open to all new experiences: day trips, subway rides into Manhattan to windowshop, dance clubs with our men and even go-go bars.

"*Chica, ¡vamos!*" she'd say to me if she saw me hold back. "No one is stopping us!"

Liliana and I became sisters and friends. Together we'd roll our eyes and laugh at Ángeles behind her back, at her theatrical ramrod rectitude and pursed lips.

We'd commemorate Mamá's death each month by gathering with family and friends in Joaquín's living room to say the full rosary for her soul, the hypnotic refrain to the protracted litany of saints—*ruega por nosotros, ruega por nosotros, ruega por nosotros*—uniting our voices in a finale of devotional humming, the sound of our stomachs growling and the younger members of the family impatiently shifting in their chairs breaking our concentration. Felipe and some of the other men would sit it out in the kitchen, drinking beers. That didn't sit well with the hosts.

"Oh, so now he's an atheist on top of being a drunk," Ángeles vented to me one day. "He was all about Mass when your mother asked him to go with her. What a faker. He's two-faced, Ruth. You need to check on that man's soul."

I said a little prayer to Santa Mónica, the patron saint of drunks and housewives, *ruega por nosotros*.

When I brought it to his attention, Felipe scowled at me. "Seriously, Ruth, what has religion done for you lately? When you were praying to that god to spare your mother that night, did he listen?" Without waiting for an answer, he continued, "I thought not. It's all a show, those stupid rosaries. It's old-fashioned superstition. It's for Joaquín and Ángeles to pretend they are holier than the rest of us, but they're really worse than all of us put together. The only people they think of is themselves. They're first, they're second and they're third. And you only matter to them if you can help them shine."

And then, the coup de grace: "The only knock I ever had on your mother is that she was blinded by her love for Joaquín. She created a monster."

I gasped. There was so much heresy in what he had said, openly questioning God's and Joaquín's motives, out loud. I had never heard anyone talk like that about either of them! My reaction was probably not what Felipe had in mind. Quietly, I began to think that maybe, just maybe, Joaquín had a point about Felipe. Although my oldest brother was an enthusiastic participant in the party Felipe created wherever he went, in private, he felt Felipe was too irreverent, too frivolous. He never said this to me in so many words; that's what Ángeles was for. He'd let her acerbic tongue do the talking for them both.

Coming face-to-face with heresy for the first time confused me. Felipe had been my first everything, from love to life. He was my first and only boyfriend. First and only lover. First date, first person to take me dancing, first person to take me on vacation. He was the first person in my life to allow me levity, to let me enjoy the pleasures of life without the onerous burdens of having to always think of the needs of others. He promised that we could be whoever we wanted to be with each other.

Maybe I had been too drunk with freedom to realize that by straying so far from my upbringing, I was threatening our souls and abdicating my responsibility to drag my husband on the straight and narrow throughout our lives, with heaven as our goal.

❧ ❧ ❧

After a month in the hospital and rehab center, Felipe came home. The doctors decided to treat the cancer directly, before doing a brain biopsy, because they had ruled out every other possible ailment. Felipe's co-workers had been checking in on him throughout, and like most other well-wishers, were uncomfortable with reality and would assure him that he'd be back out there with them in no time. Felipe loved that fiction and embraced it. He'd become impatient after every seizure—and there were too many to count—berating the doctors for not getting the drug cocktail right, arguing that he needed to be back at the office by the next week or the week after that or the week after that.

Not even the doctors had the courage to tell him the truth. He would likely never be going back to work. If the cancer proved to be grade II, which meant it would have invaded other areas in the brain and would be impossible to remove entirely, the unpredictability of the seizures meant that at 57, Felipe would be an invalid, unable to work. His salary would be courtesy of the Social Security Administration: disability insurance. To say that we were not prepared for this financial situation would be an understatement. When Felipe was 42, the shirt factory moved overseas. Felipe became the head of floor sales at their shop in town. Commissions plus salary were still respectable, but just five years later, sales had fallen so much that Felipe was let go. The writing had been on the wall, but I guess we refused to read it. We were taken by surprise. The good life is costly, and we had few savings. I went back to what I knew and took in sewing. Felipe hated me working to help pay the bills, but the bills had to be paid, so I ignored his feelings. The result was that we were either bickering or just not talking. I'd save the work for nighttime after cooking, cleaning and minding the kids or ferrying them here and there. I'd sit at my machine while watching the late-night television shows and crawl into bed after midnight. He'd be snoring. It was a challenge to our marriage.

Felipe worked one shitty job after the other for a few years until my many prayers were answered, and he got a job at the Ethan Allen furniture company sourcing fabric and preparing for its manufacturing debut in Latin America. San Cayetano, patron saint of the unemployed, *ruega por nosotros*.

The job paid a good salary that barely made a dent in the huge amount of debt we'd acquired in the interim. He was afforded a company car and lots of international travel, where his charm and good looks sealed deals and got chicks.

His philandering was the marriage killer.

Now, seeing his unfounded hopes at returning to work broke my heart. I didn't know how to break it to him that he would never be going back. Because he was still unsteady, he'd have me dial the office for him, so he could chat with his co-workers. When we were out on an errand, he'd have me drive to the office, so he could visit with them. The first few times, I could tell they were all genuinely happy to see him and would drop what they were doing to come over and chat with him. But later, their faces would flash straight-up pity or even annoyance when he'd drop in unannounced. They became "busy" if he would call and wouldn't connect with him. Felipe didn't seem to notice. I'm the one who saw it and, like a mother protecting her child, I eventually stopped dialing for him and would only very, very occasionally drive him to the office. I angered him but did so willingly because I could not stand to see him being rejected.

One evening in the early days of the cancer diagnosis, Joaquín and Ángeles drove out to visit us. As usual, they were full of platitudes about God testing us and that all would be

better in no time. They meant well. And, as usual, Joaquín
showed off his success by slipping a hundred-dollar bill under
his after-dinner coffee and winking at me, telling me to use
it to buy the grandkids Happy Meals. Ángeles would pretend
not to see it happening.

This little custom had started around the time Felipe had
lost his job. While Felipe's star was waning, Joaquín's was
rising. Not only had he become the maître d, he'd used his
and Tony's combined savings to open a Latin American fine
dining place in Forest Hills, which Tony ran, catering to rich
liberals who had spent a semester or been in the Peace Corps
in some impoverished country south of the border and loved,
absolutely loved, Tony's "authenticity" and that of his staff of
recent arrivals—cousins who had overstayed their visas. By
then, both of my brothers had moved to Westbury on Long
Island and were indulging in the middle-class suburban life
that I had beat them to years earlier.

Soon after Felipe had been let go from the Gant shirt
factory, when it became evident that similarly well-paying
jobs were going to be nearly impossible to find, I went behind
Felipe's back to ask Joaquín for a loan to tide us over.

He scoffed. "That *chavalo* has wasted every last dime
he's made, and for what? Nice cars, vacations, a house on the
beach. Did he ever think of saving? Did he ever think of his
kids' futures? I've been busting my ass here, living in the
same apartment for way too long, putting my kids through
Catholic school so they learn traditional morals and not some
soggy American ideas, putting money away for tomorrow,
and he thinks he can ask me to bail him out?" Speaking
through tight lips and pounding the table, he concluded, "That
*hijueputa* has some nerve."

"He doesn't even know I'm here, Joaquín," I squeaked.
"And please, please don't tell him I've come. It's just that I'm

worried. We've worked so hard to get where we are, and I don't want to start sliding backward. I've taken in sewing, too."

He looked hard at me. "*¡Maricón!* Making his wife work because he won't," he said. "I'm not going to help, Ruth. It's for your own good."

I said nothing.

"I've seen this before," Joaquín said. "You're becoming Mamá, may God have her in his glory. She enabled Papá all her life, springing to his rescue, and then I was the one who had to pay the price. It was always left to me to find a way to bail him out and protect you young ones. And where did that get her? She died before her time, and he got to outlive her with not a care in the world because he had his kids to keep him cozy. No, Ruth, I'm not going to let that happen to you."

Ángeles, who had probably been listening to every word from the kitchen, took that as her cue to come sidle up next to him on the couch and put her arm through his. They were a unit. She gave me a look of theatrical pity and shrugged, as if to say, "Nothing I can do about this."

On my way home, I stopped by Tony's and told him what had happened. In his usual manner, he quietly went to his room, came back with a checkbook and wrote me a $5,000 check. He said we could pay it back when we were back on our feet again. Liliana followed him out and gave me a big hug.

"You'll get through this, *chica*. We're here with you," she said. "Let us know anything you or the kids need. And don't worry, your secret is safe with us."

After that, Joaquín became showily generous at family gatherings, stuffing $20 bills of Happy Meal money into our teenagers' hands or offering Felipe and me hundred-dollar bills while still within view and earshot of others. Felipe always demurred, mumbling something positive about his latest shitty job. I took the money. Maybe Joaquín had repented of his harshness toward me and needed to work off his guilt. Maybe it was his way of apologizing. In any case, we needed it, if only to use it to make a payment on Tony's generosity.

∾∾∾

About five years after Mamá died, Papá said he was going to sell the Río Tiribí property his father had given him, plus some additional adjacent land he had inherited when his parents had died. Tony was tasked with going to Costa Rica with him to put all the paperwork in order. Joaquín had given Tony some specific tasks with regards to sales price and distribution of proceeds, details I was not privy to. But behind Tony's back, Papá went to see an old friend, an attorney, and had the property legally split in half. The house and yard and some more land all the way to the river became one property, and the inherited adjacent land, with some chicken coops, goat pens, coffee plants and a worker's shack that had been used over the years by one or another relative down on their luck or needing to dry out, became a second property. To Lucía, Papá gifted the first property, which she and her family had been living in since we had all left Costa Rica. The second property he sold, and the total price was way less than Joaquín, I'm sure, had anticipated, since the real value had been with the house and yard that faced the street. Each of us–Joaquín, Lucía, Tony and I–received $3,000 from the sale.

Felipe and I took advantage of the windfall and added it to our meager savings to scrape together a down payment for a little house near the beach. Tony and Liliana tucked theirs away into savings.

Joaquín grumbled about the unfairness of it all, and Ángeles told anyone who would listen what an ingrate her father-in-law was, how he had taken advantage of his oldest son, who had been instrumental in his family's success and instead favored the lazy Lucía and her shameless husband. The noise made it all the way to Lucía, who was very contrite about receiving Papá's favor and offered us all her $3,000 to divide amongst us, saying that she could understand Ángeles' anger. We all demurred, and Papá told her to ignore Ángeles' sharp tongue. He even sprung for a ticket to have Lucía come for a visit to put the acrimony behind us.

It was the day before Lucía was to return to Costa Rica, at a farewell dinner at his place, that Joaquín made the public announcement. "Lucía, Ángeles and I want you to know that we are so happy that Papá has rewarded you with the house that holds so many wonderful memories of the old country for us who are so far away. We know what we are and always will be sons and daughters of *la patria*. Costa Rica is in our veins. God is in our hearts. The house in San Francisco and our loyalty to this family made us who we are today.

"In fact," he went on to add, "we think that it's too bad that he didn't give you the whole lot to ensure a good financial future for your kids. So, we want you to have our share."

And with that, he and Ángeles together handed her a fat envelope stuffed with cash. It was $3,000, I suppose, although it really didn't matter how much. The guests gasped, and the room erupted in applause.

Felipe looked at me, raised his eyebrows, looking truly amused, and whispered with a chuckle, "Well that makes us look like jerks."

Lucía looked mortified. Tony kept his head down.

"Isn't he something!" one of the guests said loudly about Joaquín and raised his glass to him. A round of *salud* made its way through the room.

Another guest pulled me aside later and said, "Your mother, may she rest in peace, always knew he was a saint. You're a lucky family to have him as your brother."

Later, in private, I confessed to Lucía that I wished I could offer her my take but that it was impossible since it was tied up in the house purchase.

"Don't be an idiot, Ruth," Lucía snapped at me. "I'll never be able to repay him this. It will follow me until the day I die."

Years later, her three barely adult children banded together and convinced her to sell that old wooden house and land when developers started snapping up all the surrounding properties by the river in 1979. The sounds of birds and roosters and the river disappeared, replaced with razed lots and cement and rebar. The area was re-christened Urbanización Florestal, and like the many new subdivisions popping up all over the country, promised a new kind of tranquility and progress in the shape of urbanization and cinder-block construction. Lucía bought a modern house closer to the main road, and her children helped her pay it off well into their adulthoods.

As Lucía had predicted at the party, the debt to Joaquín and Ángeles would never be repaid. Ángeles used Lucía's adult kids' gesture to point out to everyone that, were it not for her Joaquín's early intervention and generosity toward them, they would have amounted to nothing, and instead, look how successful they had become!

∽∽∽

After stabilizing for some three months, Felipe was scheduled for a biopsy. His daily condition had leveled off, but seizures were still frequent. The drugs made him sleepy and numbed his intellect. Discussions about politics, culture and ideas were a thing of the past. And drinking would cause seizures, so Felipe was truly, finally, totally sober. That sobriety was a revelation that unmasked the real Felipe. Underneath the alcohol-induced hubris and gregariousness lived a worried, obsessive man-child. Felipe post-tumor often spent large chunks of his days massaging his anxiety about things like the weather. The kids would look at me, chagrinned, after he'd say to them, "Be careful out there today. It's going to rain."

The biopsy proved Grade II astrocytoma. The doctors were able to trim the tiny beast in his brain, but as anticipated, they were unable to remove it entirely. Instead, they said, they'd shrunken it and were going to attack the rest of it with radiation. The goal was a pre-seizure state, but they warned that we should not set our sights too high; fewer seizures would be a "success." They tempered our expectations by warning that the type of tumor Felipe had could grow faster and be more aggressive with time. In other words, they said, it wasn't over.

Even so, after two more weeks in rehab, Felipe was somewhat recharged, full of hope that life as he knew it would return. One of the first things he did was call the office to announce his imminent return. No one took his call. Instead, they sent a group card wishing him well. Felipe opened it, read it and immediately relegated it to the second drawer of his desk, where he would put whatever he didn't know what to do with, including unpaid bills. He claimed a headache, took a pill and went to sleep.

In efforts to keep him occupied and not thinking about his job, I started having him help me with the daily chores: washing dishes, making the bed, vacuuming. In the evening, we'd retreat to the den, where we listened to music and chatted while I sewed. Sometimes, he'd help sort buttons and zippers. We became a team.

On bad days, when he was especially anxious, he'd have me put the kids on speaker phone during our den time so he could warn them of impending rain or wind or heat. In return, the kids would make conversation with us both about their lives, their kids, their jobs, the news. I appreciated that.

On good days, Felipe and I would talk . . . more than we'd ever talked before. He was more reflective than he ever had been. In the past, talking about his youth in Costa Rica brought a dismissive gesture from him. He'd complain that my family focused and talked too much about the past without re-cognizing that even Costa Rica wasn't trapped in amber: it was progressing. He was forward looking, he'd say. He was an American now, he'd say, and didn't believe in wallowing about the past or in rehashing stories of friends and family we'd left behind. "That sort of thing keeps you trapped in a cage of nostalgia," he'd often say to my annoyance.

He was finally coloring in the pages of his life, about his poverty, his brother, his friends, his girlfriends, his mostly absentee mother.

"Look at that disgusting piece of shit pederast," he spat at the television news one evening. There was a segment about ongoing sexual abuse cases in the Bridgeport archdiocese and the picture of one of the accused priests came on the screen.

"Pederast?" I asked. "I don't think I've ever heard that word."

"*Pederasta*," he translated, spitting out the emphasis he put on the word as if I'd recognize it in Spanish. I didn't. He flashed me an impatient look.

"The only time my mother ever came to my defense was when she scratched Don Simón's face at San Antonio Church, the time we lived in Guadalupe. She had begged him to let me be an altar boy, telling him that I had the voice of an angel. Despite her reputation, he took me on, but only because he liked fucking little boys," Felipe said, his gaze distant.

"As soon as she left me there," Felipe continued, "he started telling me how pretty I was. Then he closed the door to the sacristy and had me sing for him. He told me to come back every day because I had a lot of catching up to do. I did what he said. Every day after school, I'd go straight to San Antonio's, in the back door, into the sacristy. He'd be waiting for me with a milky coffee and a sweet roll. I'd sing for him, and he'd tell me how pretty I was and how beautiful my voice was and how someday I'd make an excellent priest. Then he started hugging me. Then . . ." He stopped his story abruptly.

"Did he . . . ?" I asked, alarmed.

He didn't answer.

"I kept going after that for a while. Mamá was so happy about me being an altar boy, even though she wouldn't set foot in a church. Saúl would tease me, calling me a faggot, but he didn't know anything. He just was making fun of my high voice. He also didn't go to church and would grab me in a headlock and scrape his knuckles across my head, calling me 'Little Don Felipe.' I think he was proud of me, even though he made fun of me.

"But then I started skipping Don Simón's 'lessons.' Mamá didn't notice because she was never home. But he saw her on the corner one day, selling her tortillas as usual, and he went to grub a freebie. 'I haven't seen Felipe in a week,' he said. 'I knew he'd be a loser, because, well, his family . . .' he said to her.

"Mamá was furious with me that night. She had barely walked in the door when her arms were flailing, looking for their target in me. 'Felipe, you good for nothing,' she scream-ed. 'You've shamed me. You couldn't even keep your commit-ment to Don Simón.'

"At the sound of his name, my face crumbled and the tears that didn't flow from the beating now wouldn't stop. Mamá stopped and grabbed me by both arms. 'Did he . . . did he hurt you?' She didn't wait for an answer. She grabbed my arm and dragged me down the street to San Antonio's and barged into the rectory, shoving past the housekeeper, screaming for Don Simón to get there that instant. He came out, a napkin wiping crumbs from his fat face. He smiled when he saw us. 'So, you spoke some sense to your pretty little son?' he managed to get out before she dropped my arm and, like a mad cat, set upon his face with her nails and screeching that he would rot in hell, that he was a faggot and scum, the lowest of the low, a devil. I stood by, stunned. The housekeeper didn't move, only lowered her head as Mamá screamed out the obscene accusations. It took only seconds for Don Simón to respond and defend himself from my much smaller mother, but by then the damage was done. His face was adorned with a dozen ribbons of red blood.

"And just as fast as it started, Mamá stepped back, grabbed my arm again and dragged me to the door. Before she left, she turned around and said to him: 'Explain that face now, you son of a whore!' To cap off her attack, she inhaled and then launched the juiciest gob of spit right on his nose.

"I was eight. I spent the rest of that winter trying to spit as far and juicy as she had."

I had so many questions. I couldn't ask them. I was struck dumb by Felipe's story. In the end, he was smiling slightly, remembering his mother's heroics, and he chuckled.

"You know, Don Simón died of old age, still master of his title and parish. People knew what he was, but back then no one did anything about it. And that son-of-a-bitch must have been a talker, because so many guys seemed to know me, caress my cheek and call me pretty. When I was older, they straight-up propositioned me, offering me food or a job in return."

I never bothered to ask if hunger or desperation led him to accept their offers. I didn't want to know. It didn't matter.

Later that week, Amalia came by with the kids, who always perked Felipe up, especially her littlest one. He would clamber up on his *abuelito*'s lap, not grasping Felipe's fragility and entertain him with childish songs or elaborate incomprehensible stories that he'd improvise on the spot. Felipe would laugh and egg him on, never begging out of it because of a headache or fatigue or any other of his daily symptoms. The only reason to scoot the toddler away was for fear of a seizure, which Felipe would warn of with a sharp "Ruth!"– my cue.

"Remember that day at Denny's, when your dad talked about the governor?" I asked Amalia after we sat down with our coffees at the kitchen table.

She didn't look up, just mumbled her assent.

"Felipe's not gay, you know. We were talking the other day, and he told me about some problems he had with a priest when he was little."

"You mean pedophile problems, Mom?" Her tone was sharp. "Geez, you just found out now? No wonder he hated church. I'd have stayed far away, too. How could you not know about this until now?"

I didn't bother to answer. How could I not know about it? Some things were unknowable.

Amalia was pensive, sipping her coffee.

"You know, Mom, he could still be both, and that's not a reflection on you. It's obvious he likes women, besides you, of course." She let her voice trail off, not wanting to speak the unspeakable.

For years, since he became an international traveling salesman, Felipe had not been secretive enough about his dalliances with other women. The kids were all in college and I was busy being family organizer, housewife, dressmaker, mother. Felipe would take off on some trip or other, barely call, come home with his dirty clothes neatly folded but smelling of perfume, and I'd wash them. The few times I called him out on it, we had incredible blow-outs. He'd accuse me of being a hysteric and a jealous idiot. Then he'd threaten to leave because I stifled him, or bored him, and he'd sneeringly challenge me to go talk it out with Joaquín or pray with my brother for my husband to find the straight and narrow.

I never talked to Joaquín about Felipe's shortcomings. I didn't have to. He knew all about it because, as he'd openly say, he knew a million guys like Felipe. They'd come to the restaurant acting like big shots with a young women on their arms and company American Express cards in their wallets. They'd lavish these women with the attention they couldn't spare for their middle-aged wives at home. Joaquín would cluck his tongue and make a fist and say, "Someday your *chavalo* is going to get what he deserves." Ángeles, who was never far from the conversation, would silently nod in agreement. But at family gatherings, Joaquín would be all laughs and glad-hand Felipe, and neither would challenge the other.

To Tony and Liliana, I'd reveal little truths occasionally, but they wouldn't pile on. "Ruth, do what you have to do," he'd say, never letting on what he thought I should do, stay or leave, tell him off or keep silent. Liliana would say, "Chica, it's your life," and remain neutral, too. With Lucía, I could commiserate, but commiseration brings misery times two, so at the height of the problems with his other women, I'd avoid talking with her.

47

I could see that Amalia had more to say, but while she hesitated, I felt the need to defend Felipe.

"You know, honey, he didn't have any positive examples in life. His mother, well, when she did bother to be there, she would be carousing with whichever man would pay her month's rent and food. And those men were all probably married and throwing around their extra cash to impress some poor, desperate chick who was cute and could pretend to care a little bit about him," I explained. "We had a name for women like her: *flor de la noche*, a night flower."

"But he could be both, Mom. You've always said jokes reveal hidden truths, and Dad always has been quick to make a gay joke, even if he claims to have only respect for gay men because he's worked with so many. Maybe some of those so-called other women of his have been men, and that was his way of telling us. I almost feel bad for him! Can you imagine how hard it would be to keep it in all these years? It's not like you'd be, um, open about it. You're not, you know, sexually liberated. I don't blame you! You were raised . . ."

"No," I said flatly. "Don't be dramatic. I'm his wife. I'd know."

We dropped the topic. But in the recesses of my brain, it wouldn't quit. Could I have missed it? Was I a fool, or had my fidelity been a form of compassion, allowing him to become the new man he always wanted to be? Should I ask him about it? If I did, would he even remember telling me about Don Simón. If I reminded him that he'd told me the story, would it embarrass him? The louder chorus in my head would say, "It doesn't matter. Let it be."

I never brought it up again.

Felipe had to have a second surgery at month eight. Despite the radiation, the tumor had continued to grow, and there was evidence that it might have jumped its original borders to create a new spot nearby. That's why he had begun to have so many small seizures again.

The night before the surgery, we were in his hospital room, and he started to cry. I'd seen him cry before, drunk and stupid, but these were big, ugly, sober tears. Once he started, it seemed like he couldn't stop.

"This wasn't how it was supposed to be," he bawled. "I had plans."

I couldn't help wondering if those plans had included me, but I didn't let the question escape. All I could say was, "I know." And I did know. Felipe had often said he would never retire, especially not after rising from the ashes and landing such a wonderful job, the sort of job he would only have dreamed of as a young man. But in the past couple of years, he had also let me know in so many ways that I was in his way, that I was a drag on his happiness. Yet, all that seemed so far away now. In his convalescence over that year, we had become inseparable . . . mostly out of necessity, since I had become his driver, his daily assistant and, really, his only friend. Our routine was not unlike that from early motherhood: waking, breakfast, chores, showers, nap time for him, then a late lunch that bled into the evening news and music sometimes, if he was feeling up to it. During his waking time, if it was a good day, we'd chat about the past, the kids' futures, the grandkids or politics. The kids worried about me; they kept telling me to hire someone to dad-sit every now and then, so that I could have some time to myself. But, besides the expense, which we could definitely not afford without Felipe's job, I didn't want to. I was enjoying the new-old Felipe. He was reminding me of the twenty-year-old who crossed the country to sit with me in my family's living room and had opened up my world.

I didn't hate his tumor. I felt that it had given us a second chance. If not for it, I would have been rooming with Lucía, stewing in my bitterness. I thought, I really believed, that Felipe would beat it and, if not land on his feet, then at least make the most of his new normal, and we'd live happier than we had before.

They cleaned up the edges of the tumor during the second surgery and discovered that the new spot was a false alarm. They declared the surgery a success, saying the cancer might even have been rendered chronic, not deadly. But it did nothing to alleviate Felipe's anxiety, and neither, it seemed, did the medications.

One day, in a moment of rare clarity the week after he came home from the hospital, he said to me, "Ruth, I know I'm dying. But it's not time. I'd be a fool not to fight it."

That night, he sought me out when I stepped away to pray the rosary. I'd taken to doing it privately, because I knew it bothered him that I believed in God and in the power of prayer.

"I'll say it with you," was all he said, and we started.

In the weeks that followed, the rosary became our new nightly ritual. He even pulled out a prayer card of Pope John Paul II that someone had given to him and propped it up behind the little bowl I kept my rosary in.

"That guy will hear me. He'll answer our prayers," he said of the pope.

I was stunned. Felipe had never talked like that.

"He'll be a saint soon," he said. "Miracles are coming out of the woodwork. He's been curing people of their cancer."

I had no idea where Felipe might have gotten any of that information, but I didn't contradict him. It was probably true.

And John Paul II was the only Catholic figure that Felipe ever tolerated a little. When he had come to New York in 1979, Joaquín and Ángeles had scored tickets for their whole family to see him at Yankee Stadium. But Tony, Liliana, all our kids and I stood for hours along the route to St. Patrick's to catch a glimpse of him in his popemobile. Felipe refused to stand with us, bleating at us like we were sheep, then winking and laughing. With his camera hanging from his neck, he said he'd catch us later, and took off walking up the street.

Later, elated that we had seen the pope and were able to wave our little Vatican flags at his car, we all were gathered in Tony's dining room to review the day's excitement. Felipe hadn't returned with us but had walked in late, positively beaming, and said that the pope had blessed him. Not him in a crowd of onlookers, but him, alone. He had ventured away from the crowd and found himself totally alone for a split second on a city block, and the popemobile had materialized. He and John Paul II had made eye contact, Felipe had waved and the pope made the sign of the cross with his hand in the air, blessing him.

"I'm a new man," he declared, with enough jocularity that no one took him seriously. In fact, we had a good laugh at his expense, joking that there must have been a nun standing behind him at whom the pope was aiming his blessing, or that the pope really meant to sprinkle holy water on him to get the exorcism going. Everyone laughed heartily, Felipe included.

After that papal blessing, I swear he tried to be a better man. He cut his drinking down dramatically, and he'd come straight home from work. Then he stopped drinking altogether. That period coincided with my birthday. We invited the usual suspects: Tony, Liliana, Joaquín, Ángeles, the kids and our local friends. It was a small gathering, and it was unusually subdued that year. Felipe stuck to ginger ales. Joaquín noticed.

"My God, what happened to you? Did the doctor tell you you're dying?" he said, joking, to Felipe and opened a beer bottle and handed it to him.

"Nah, not tonight. I'm giving my liver a rest," Felipe joked back, waving off the bottle.

"Get outta here! It's Ruth's birthday. You need to toast her!"

I stepped into the conversation to save Felipe and said, "Hey, Joaquín, let him be."

I really appreciated the hiatus on booze. It had been peaceful at home, and I think we were both happy about it.

But Joaquín wasn't quitting. He again handed Felipe a beer, and this time, Felipe accepted it and took a swig.

I walked away, annoyed that my brother, the brother who had long railed about Felipe's drinking, had ruined his dry streak. I was so mad, in fact, that I actually brought it up the next day in a phone conversation with Joaquín.

"What the hell, Joaquín? You have been criticizing his drinking since before we were even married, and yesterday you were like a drug pusher."

"Calm down, Ruth. It was one beer. It's not going to kill him."

"You're a hypocrite!" I cried. "You and Ángeles constantly draw attention to his failings, to his weakness with liquor. He decides to rise above it, and you just shove him down again. Why would you do that?"

"Leave Ángeles out of this. She doesn't even drink. And besides, the party was getting too quiet. Felipe, I mean, let's face it, he was boring last night."

I didn't know what to say to that. Felipe was boring, I guess. But at the end of the night, when the guests had left, we sat and chatted about nothing in particular, maybe music or rehashing the night. It was enjoyable, maybe like vanilla ice cream, but that's my favorite. Boring was great, for a change.

Joaquín had the last word, as usual.

"Listen, Ruth, you know what you married. If he really wants to stop drinking, he will stop drinking, and no one, not me, not you, will be able to tempt him. He needs to be his own man if he even is enough of a man."

I thought about it and decided he wasn't wrong. Mamá had harangued Papá every day and every night about his drinking, and then one day, after a particularly bad binge, Papá just stopped and never looked back. It didn't matter that his brothers and friends and everyone around him still boozed. He didn't. Never again.

With that in mind, one evening after Felipe came home from work, I asked him to open a bottle of wine and pour me a glass. He did. Then he downed the rest of the bottle by himself. Maybe it's hindsight or projection, but I swear now that he looked at me that night with a combination of anger and despair.

∾ ∾ ∾

The canonization process of John Paul II became Felipe's new obsession. Every night he'd prop up the little laminated prayer card and join me in the rosary. Then, he heard about the Costa Rican lawyer—the third miracle—who was cured of a tumor or an aneurysm or something like that. Ángeles had told him about it. According to her, Floribeth Mora Díaz had watched the beatification ceremony on TV, mortally ill, and dreamt that the pope told her to get up. When she did, she was cured. When he heard that, Felipe became more obsessed. He, too, was Costa Rican. He, too, was mortally ill! He, too, had been blessed by John Paul II! He could be the fourth miracle! It would be win-win for them: Felipe would be saved, and John Paul II would get his halo.

I had misgivings. Miracles weren't supposed to be transactional like that. But then, why not? Maybe Felipe could be saved, even though Ángeles made sure to note that his litany of sins would likely preclude him from Floribeth's fate. He would need to confess, I reminded him. He scoffed. He hadn't been to confession since he was Don Simón's altar boy and didn't plan on confessing now. Well, contrition then, I said.

"For what?" he deadpanned.

Amalia and Eddie were there when he said that. They both laughed out loud, thinking their father was joking.

Felipe looked aggrieved. "Really, for what? Have I been a bad person? Didn't I make the most out of life? Wasn't I a good father? I worked, I made sure you got ahead, got you everything you needed and more. Really, what do you think makes me a bad candidate for a miracle?"

"Well, Dad, I mean, there's Mom . . ." Eddie started. "I mean, you could have been better, maybe?"

After five years, the newness had not worn off Eddie's marriage. He worked hard to be a good husband, a good father, conscientious and dedicated. I didn't doubt that it was in reaction to the example he had grown up with. But even so, it was shocking to me to hear him criticize his father. He had never challenged his father's behavior before.

"Better? Oh yeah, you think?" challenged Felipe. "Name one way, I dare you."

Emboldened, Eddie said, "Well, there's the other women for starters."

I couldn't stand it. I always feared this type of con-frontation. "Enough," I scolded Eddie. "Leave your dad alone. Everybody knows what's in their souls. That's between them and God."

I shut up when I saw, out of the corner of my eye, Amalia roll her eyes.

∾ ∾ ∾

When Felipe had been sick for nearly two years, Joaquín and Ángeles went on vacation to Rome and the Vatican, with a special invitation for a mass audience with the new pope, set up by their parish priest, who was forever holding them up as singular examples of Catholic parents, thanks to their kids graduating from the parish school and their never having missed weekly donations.

Upon their return, they visited us bearing holy water from the Vatican and a new Pope John Paul II prayer card laminated with a tiny relic from his white papal cassock. They presented both to Felipe. They gave me a new rosary. That night, they joined us in saying the rosary.

When I walked them to the door, I was genuinely grateful for their visit, their gifts.

"Your *chavalo* is really turning a new leaf, huh? What's the saying? There are no atheists in foxholes," Joaquín said. "It's too bad he didn't try this out years ago when it might have made a difference."

Ángeles nodded and patted my hand.

Less than a month later, Joaquín was dead. He had dropped dead at work, after first clutching his chest, like Mamá did, and falling face down in the restaurant. His funeral was not unlike Mamá's. So many people showed up, many whose faces I had never seen. The wailing and keening were so intense and loud that for an irreverent second, I suspected Ángeles had hired professional mourners. Poor Ángeles was destroyed, prostrate with grief. Joaquín had been her alpha and omega. She drew strength from his approval, and he had let her live her life uncensored. She had tormented us. Nevertheless, on the day Joaquín was buried, I only had pity for her. Who would shield her now? In her eulogy, she emphasized how at their union his goodness had enhanced her virginal virtue and turned their marriage into a long prayer. He was the best of the best, she said, and with a quick, sideways glance at the pew where we sat, she added that God always takes his saints first. The good, she said, stealing a glance at us again, always die young. Joaquín had already passed his seventieth *mañanita*. Felipe and I cried quietly, together. We sat with Tony and Liliana, who were less consolable.

After the ceremony, Felipe reached across me and shook hands with Tony. "Your brother was a good man, a great man," Felipe said, sniffling.

Tony could not look up, he was crying so much.

"Do you know what made him so great?" Felipe continued. "He was imperfect. He was so flawed, he didn't even know it, but that didn't stop him from always trying to be better. Don't forget that, man. None of us will ever be a saint, but that doesn't mean we can't pretend we are."

As we left the church, Joaquín's children handed us all personalized prayer cards featuring an image of San Joaquín– from the Hebrew meaning "he whom Yahweh has established." He was the father of Mary-mother-of-Jesus and the patron saint of fathers and married couples. They designed the card to have San Joaquín arm in arm with an image of my brother. Behind my brother's head was the faintest of halos. Joaquín Jesús, *ruega por nosotros*.

❧ ❧ ❧

It was not long after Joaquín's death that Felipe asked me to take him to Costa Rica. We had been back occasionally over the years for visits, but always at my request. Felipe would oblige but remind me that we were the lucky ones. We had been given a second chance at life to reinvent ourselves as Americans. Our home was here now. Our sights were supposed to be set perpetually on the horizon. When we'd get there, he'd call on old friends and ask them to show us the newest, hottest bars and discos. We'd take the kids to nature parks and sites we'd never seen before, and he'd tell them they should be proud of Costa Rica, even if their Spanish was poor. We always had good trips and returned to Connecticut more grounded, surer of ourselves. I'm sure he knew this would be his last visit.

Whether we could afford it or not was never a question we asked ourselves. Disability payments helped some but did not go far enough. I had picked up the sewing work, and it helped pay the bills. Felipe would keep me company while I worked, often giving design advice or helping sort buttons and spools or ironing garments. In time, I figured, Social Security retirement payments would kick in for all of Felipe's years of hard work; plus all the times I had lent my Social Security number to some cousin or other trying her luck in the US would amount to a little sum to see us through our old age. In any case, I believed the kids wouldn't let us eat dog food. They were good.

We didn't pack bathing suits because we didn't plan on leaving San Jose for a beach trip. It was a chance to see whoever was left behind, especially Saúl and Lucía. Once we had arrived, Saúl made ample time to hang out with his kid brother and, after reminiscing boisterously about their rowdy youth, he became subdued. The two brothers had tender-looking tête-à-têtes by lamplight that left Felipe wistful and quiet. I was not privy to their discussion. We slept at Lucía's, in the house her kids had helped her buy, up the way from where we had grown up. Lucía and Felipe had always gotten along, as both had generous personalities when it came to others. Felipe was drawing on some unknown reserve of energy and would stay up into the wee hours with her, drinking coffee and eating her homemade rolls at all hours of the night. One night, toward the end of our stay, I over-heard their conversation in the living room from where I was reading a magazine.

"Douglas was terrible," Felipe said. It was uncharacteristic of him to make such ugly, opinionated declarations to people he liked. "He didn't deserve you and he sure as shit didn't deserve the kids you gave him. Brutes like him have no business thinking they can be family men."

"He wasn't all bad," Lucía said.

Widowed for more than fifteen years by then, she had indulged in revisionist history when it came to Douglas, slowly transforming him from a louse into a simply flawed man, a human being.

"Sometimes he tried."

"You mean, 'sometimes he tried' to kill you. Or 'some-times he tried' to beat the brains out of his kids. Or 'sometimes he tried' to steal from more people, besides just his family and friends," Felipe said, laughing lightly to try to make a joke of it. But he meant every word he said. "I would have not thought badly of you at all if you had walked away from him. Shit! I would have defended you if you had killed him in his sleep!"

Lucía was quiet for a long minute. When she spoke, her voice was soft and a little hesitant. "What would you have thought if Ruth had left you?" she asked him.

"Come on! You can let go. You can admit that he was a son of a whore," Felipe said.

"She almost did, you know. She almost left you," Lucía said with a little more force.

I held my breath.

"What? Come on! Why?"

"It's true. I told her to come to me. I told her to leave you. I told her you didn't deserve her. She almost did it, too," Lucía told him. "But then, you got sick, and she couldn't."

I felt sick to my stomach. I wanted to run in there and put an end to her confessions, my confessions. I wanted to scream, "Stop! Erase that! He's changed!"

But I didn't move.

In the next room, there was silence for a few beats, and then Felipe spoke. "Why would you say that, that I didn't deserve her? I was a good husband! I always made sure she had a roof over her head, pretty things to wear, good food to eat. I was a good father. The kids are happy, they're successful. I had nothing growing up, and I gave them everything. Why would she have ever considered leaving me?" he said, almost plaintively. "I don't know whether to believe you or not, Lucía."

"You were a jerk to her! All those other women . . ."

"The women meant nothing! Every man dallies," he protested. "It was the liquor. I never cheated sober. I swear."

"You didn't even try to hide them. You didn't try to pretend for her sake. You just dangled them in front of her, like an ugly penis. And then you'd humiliate her, drinking yourself into THAT guy and harassing women IN FRONT OF HER. Can you imagine how she might have felt? I would have hit you in the balls if you had done that to me. I used to put rocks in my purse so that I could beat on Douglas when he came home smelling of other women. . . ."

They both hooted in laughter when she said this. I imagined them holding their sides, the laughter not stopping, both of them gasping for air. The laughter came as relief, diffusing the accusations she was leveling at him.

When it finally subsided into chuckles and they had broken the spell by drinking water, Lucía continued. "She's always loved you. You told her so often when you were drunk that you would be leaving her in the future. You'd put her on notice," Lucía said, somber again. "You'd break her heart over and over and over again. And she still couldn't stop loving you."

"I knew the women bothered her," he admitted to my sister. "But I also thought she knew it was only her. I drank too much. But it was only ever her."

"Joaquín once said . . ." she began.

"Stop. Don't bring up Joaquín. He poisoned Ruth against me. We're all imperfect, but he, may he rest in peace, took out his shit, his insecurities on me. There was a time, in the beginning, when Ruth thought I was the sun and the moon . . . and then Joaquín got jealous because even Mamá liked me, and he spent way too much of his time pointing out my flaws to her . . . to lessen his own insecurities."

"You're not wrong, Felipe. Joaquín, may God have him in his glory, didn't hate you. You were very different from him . . . he had been raised to see only one way as the right way, his way. Mamá made sure we all knew he was destined to lead and we to follow. We let her because it made her happy to think that she had given birth to a real-life saint, San Joaquín Jesús. I think Joaquín really believed he would for sure go to heaven if he colored in the lines, which he did. Telling him otherwise would have been heresy! And look, his life was well ordered. He succeeded at his career, he made money, his kids are lovely, his wife . . ." Lucía paused for a second. "Good Lord, his wife! Imagine having to share a bed with that woman for decades and daily pretend that you didn't make a huge, irreversible mistake when you were in your twenties!"

At that, they both cracked up again, snorting and, from the sound of it, one of them falling off their chair in hysterics.

∾ ∾ ∾

Upon our return home, there was a huge change for me. Without Joaquín around, I felt free to indulge Felipe. I no longer found myself dedicating my prayers and penance toward changing him. Now, I just found myself praying for his cancer to be stopped in its tracks so that we could make up for time lost—time lost bickering, time lost in jealousy, time lost trying to make him over in the image of Joaquín.

I regretted that I had not been easier on Felipe, that I had tried to cage his spirit in the hopes of saving his soul. I lamented that instead of taking him by the hand and running barefoot through life. I had insisted that he try to confine himself to life as I knew it: purposeful, planned, with the service of others as a goal.

One anniversary, when the kids were still little, before the other women came along, Felipe gave me a caged finch as a gift. It was an adorable little bird that would sing along to the Saturday morning music and added background to the kids' play and laughter. When he gave the caged bird to me, he set it on the sideboard and opened the little sliding door on the cage.

"Let's let this little guy find his freedom," he said to me, winking at the wide-eyed children. "He'll always know where to come for food and a bed, but the whole house can be his playground."

For a couple of years, the little bird enjoyed the good life, hopping from plant to plant throughout the day, perching itself on the piano, if one of the children was playing it, or finding its way to the kitchen to pick the seeds off the pepper heart I'd leave on the table for it.

I truly believed the little bird was the happiest bird on earth: free but protected by us.

One mild June afternoon, when the warm sea breeze was wafting in and the smell of salt was in the air, I opened the dining room window wide and went about my chores, intoxicated by the summer. I had forgotten that the little bird was aloft in the house. Amalia was the one who remembered, at dusk, when she came in from the yard and saw the dining room sheer curtains flapping and the door of the cage wide open.

"Mom! How could you?" she accused me.

The little bird was nowhere to be found, not in the plants or on the piano or in the kitchen.

I burst out crying. Felipe, who had been setting the table for dinner, also hadn't noticed.

He came over and consoled us both. "Don't cry," he had said. "If he comes back, he comes back. If he doesn't, wish him a good and adventurous life in the big world out there."

And then, just to Amalia, he added, "There is so much to do out there, more than just one lifetime's worth of fun."

I wondered if Joaquín had enough fun. If all you know is your cage, and it's a nice cage, can't that be enough for a happy life? He had hit all the benchmarks: a wife who loved him, successful children, financial success. And yet, I couldn't help feeling a little badly for him and wondering why it had been so important to him to end up on top, the best of the best, a saint? We had all facilitated this goal, but I had done so to the detriment, I now believed, of my one and only opportunity to escape my cage in life. Felipe had left the door open, and I never, ever thought of flying out the window.

I had wasted my life, my youth, and Felipe's as well, I now felt, trying to achieve sanctity. But for what? So my kids could make me a photoshopped prayer card when I died?

Felipe kept on praying to John Paul for a miracle.

∽∽∽

Henry began to unravel at Felipe's newfound prayerfulness. He was not unlike his father and had never entered a church he liked. Prayer was superstition, he always said to me. In the past, Felipe and he would engage in deep, philosophical discussions about life without God. If he was in the mood, Felipe would make sure I could hear the digs he'd make about people, "Like your mother's family who believed prayer not only could save you from Hell, but also could force a change in those around you. And instead of peace, they drag everyone around them into the hell on earth they create." Then he'd begin a litany of prayerful sinners he believed wasted their one chance at life. Ángeles would often get slipped in there. Joaquín, to my surprise would not.

One day, Henry eyed with suspicion his father's John Paul II shrine complete with prayer cards next to the little, plastic bottle of holy water on his night table.

"Dad, you know, as a father, I'm surprised you dig that guy so much, since he never did anything to all the priests who molested all those kids," he said. "He just let them all fade away into more obscure parishes or group homes in the desert. Those assholes all died peacefully because the pope let them. They should have gone to jail. Or he should have turned them over to the kids' fathers and let them have at them!"

Felipe stayed quiet for a little bit, then said, "Henry, you can't believe everything you read. We're all good and bad mixed together. And anyway, have you heard about his cancer cures?"

∾∾∾

Amalia managed to coordinate with her brothers to have them both hang out with Felipe while their wives watched the kids so that she and I could go out for lunch and pedicures. I wasn't really too eager, but it meant a lot to her, so I indulged her.

I think she wanted me to be her captive audience, emphasis on *captive*. It was time, she announced before the nail technician had even finished filling up the pedicure basins, to get stuff off her chest. What she needed to get off her chest was supposedly pent-up animosity toward her father because of his drinking and womanizing. If I had to judge solely by her Christmas/Birthday/Father's Day cards, gifts and all the "come with" invitations to her family trips or special outings, I would never have guessed she had pent up anything.

My skepticism must have been apparent on my face.

"If I haven't ever cut off my relationship with him before, Mom, it was because of you," she said in answer to the question I hadn't asked.

"Amalia, he wasn't a terrible father. In fact, he was pretty darn good. He'd spend every last dime of his bonuses on your Christmas gifts when you kids were little. He was your biggest cheerleader when it came to your education. Sure, he couldn't contribute to your college, but, you know, times were very tough then. He never once stopped supporting you

with a roof and food and love, even if he had trouble expressing it."

She sighed. "That's your problem, Mom. 'Gratitude' is so
ingrained in you that, so long as someone fed and housed you,
or so long as they were better than so and so's husband who
gave her black eyes or actually left her to live with some tramp,
you never bothered to ask if they were *actually* good to you,"
she said. "I'm not like you. I have issues with the way he
treated you. I get it, now is not the time to tell him, but I feel
like I'll never be able to properly get these things off my chest."

She annoyed me. Everything was so black and white for
her. The opposite of good was bad. The opposite of happy
was sad. Her pictures had dark black lines around the images,
and she spent her whole life coloring neatly within the lines.
My pictures were more like that Monet guy, blurry edges,
pretty pastel colors so that the harshness can blend away. I
always wondered how this daughter of mine turned out so
unlike me.

She continued, ". . . I mean, it would be wrong of me to
pile on him. But you don't have to be the martyr, Mom. No
matter what you do, no one is going to canonize you because
you took care of him when he was dying."

The harshness of the way she said "dying" struck me.
Deep down, I knew Felipe was dying. He was dying in the
worst way possible: wide awake, watching life slip out of his
grip, unable to do anything to stop it. Joaquín's and Mamá's
deaths on the spot were preferable. They probably didn't even
know what hit them.

Years ago, when I was still trying to coax Felipe to go to
church, he mentioned flippantly that he hoped he died in his
sleep after a fabulous night of partying. I had argued that
knowing at least a minute or two before would be better

because you could quickly make an Act of Contrition and get your soul in order before you departed.

Felipe laughed. "Shit, Ruth, when are you ever going to stop with that nonsense? Hell is only on Earth."

So now, Felipe was in what may have been his version of Hell. So, what does he do? Repent of his life of sin. He once said to me that his new greatest fear was that he had brought this disease on himself because of his years of heavy drinking, and that by doing so he may have committed the worst sin possible: wasting his life.

Surprisingly, I was annoyed at him for this, too. But not because I entirely disagreed with him. I just wanted the old Felipe back.

"I'm not going to leave him, Amalia," I said to her. "I love him. I actually like him. I always have. Despite all the bad stuff, he's a good guy. Really. You need to get over it."

"I get it, Mom. It's okay, I understand," she said, changing her voice to the soothing voice one uses on children. "Your father was an alcoholic. Your uncles were alcoholics. Most of the men you ever knew were alcoholics. And your husband is an alcoholic. Your role as a woman—as well as your mother's, your aunts', your sisters'—is to be an enabler. You're traumatized."

"Seriously, Amalia," I said, "get over yourself."

She was agape. "He could have killed us any number of times by driving drunk with us in the car," she spat out.

"But you didn't die," I answered with a shrug. Then, attempting a rapprochement, I said, "Look, here you are, getting your toes done and lecturing your mother. Life is good. Be happy."

∾∾∾

When Felipe propped up Joaquín's prayer card next to John Paul's, I deliberately skipped the rosary that night. He didn't forget. He reminded me it was time. I couldn't deny him—that would be wrong.

"I see you put Joaquín there," I noted. "Are you remembering him today?"

"Well, I need all the help I can get. If you guys were all right about his being so close to God all those years, well, maybe it won't hurt to have him put in a good word for me," Felipe said. Then, in a flash of the old Felipe, he added with a wink, "In any case, he probably wants God all to himself for a little while, so he can ask Him to put off my time so that I don't go steal the show from him."

After we said the rosary—I was uncomfortable the whole time with my brother's haloed head staring right at us—I tried to explain to Felipe some new thoughts I'd been having.

"I've been thinking about Joaquín a lot lately. About his life. How he was always so sure that he was right, that we were wrong. Especially you and I," I said. "He really, really resented that we didn't follow his rules of life that he, and maybe Mamá, thought were so important for happiness. We *were* happy regardless, weren't we? Maybe I shouldn't have been so quick to listen to his 'wisdom' all the time. I think I may have hurt us by doing that. Maybe he wasn't always right. Maybe I should have followed your lead more often."

Felipe was quietly snoring.

I continued reviewing our life together. I thought of all the times that I had judged Felipe's behavior—his *joie de vivre*, his cavorting, his heresy—through Joaquín's lens. If I ever was inclined to shrug off his behavior, I'd stop myself short, reminding myself that what he was doing was wrong and that my job in life was to live correctly and encourage that in my spouse.

I had an aunt, one of my father's younger sisters, who was closer in age to me than him. She had married a boozer, but unlike my mother, she didn't gnash her teeth and pull her hair out. She joined him whenever she could. We chatted about this during one of my trips to Costa Rica in past years. She had heard me complaining in whispers with Lucía at a family event when Felipe had gone too deep into his cups and was becoming "the life of the party," as usual.

My aunt scolded me like a child. "Quit your whining and go out there and have fun with him," she said. "Your mother and all those old ladies were ninnies, clutching their rosary beads and making lunch for the priest. They were miserable all their lives, and they made their husbands miserable. No wonder their men just drank more! You're too young for that shit. Be modern! Join him!"

That night, I did sit next to him, and I did drink a little more than usual. But I couldn't keep it up. It seemed so wrong. Life couldn't be that easy, I thought.

Now, lying next to a snoring, dying Felipe, I realized that maybe it could have been that easy. All those times that I had made us miserable trying to do the right thing, what if I had not? What if I had not been embarrassed that Felipe liked to drink so much? What if, instead of wincing and sulking when he took other women out to dance at parties, I had cut in and had fun with him instead? What if, instead of begging him to change before it was too late, I had let him enjoy his life more the way he wanted to? (If only we had known it was going to be so short.) Who, really, was watching? Who really cared what we did? These were not big-time mortal sins, like killing or stealing, but venial stuff. Drinking too much, not going to church, living like we enjoyed living . . . Who cared? What had I been so afraid of?

⁓⁓⁓

Felipe's seizures picked up in frequency and force. The doctors prescribed more and newer medication to inhibit blood supply to the cancer, but they warned about side effects. His short-term memory weakened. So did his blood vessels. There was nothing else they could do. The possibility of strokes was added to Felipe's list of anxieties.

I was completely disheartened by the prognosis, but if Felipe was also, he didn't let on.

"You'll see, John Paul will come through for me," he said, but his hand grazed Joaquín's card instead.

In those days, Felipe had been reminiscing about Joaquín a lot more than usual. He often couldn't remember that he had seen his grandchildren two days earlier, but he could recall in detail conversations he had had twenty-five years earlier. Most of his memories about my brother were positive, but occasionally he'd rue that he hadn't said this or that, or hadn't defended himself better, or that he had never called out Joaquín or Ángeles' occasional bigotry or hatefulness toward anyone not white, straight or religious.

"They were narrow-minded," he declared one day after regaling me with some long-forgotten Sunday dinner party conversation about what they would do if they thought one of their children were gay. Their plan, they said, was to send him to Costa Rica and have him held prisoner at some ranch outside of civilization until he took a wife out of sheer loneliness.

"But they were always happy," he concluded. "That's the privilege of the, well, not so smart. They really never know what they're missing." And then he added, "If you took away all their bad parts, they were actually good people."

It surprised me that Felipe had forgiven so many slights. In the year after Joaquín's death, I couldn't help but kick myself for not having seen it sooner. In order for Joaquín to become the saint he was destined to be, the rest of us had to suffer along with him. Why had it been impressed on us so often in our early education to emulate the lives of saints? How could anyone want to teach children to be like saints? We were taught to call on them in time of need. We were told to learn to live by their examples, which were supposed to ease our lives in difficult times. When my sister was forced to give up Isaac, in between beatings, she was reminded of her name saint: Santa Lucía, who had dedicated her virginity to God and rebuffed a suitor, then had her eyes gouged out before she was killed. When we misbehaved or complained as children, it was St. Dominic Savio we were reminded of before we were spanked: he declared at age seven that his only friends would be Jesus and Mary and that he'd rather die than sin. He was only fourteen when pleurisy took him, dying before really living. Or St. Therese of Liseux, the Little Flower of Jesus, orphaned when she was four and then at fifteen begged and begged to enter the convent that all of her older sisters had joined. Mamá would remind me of her when I cried about having to work and not being allowed to go to school like other kids my age. She'd say that St. Therese was so holy she didn't want to waste time living in the world. But maybe she was just lonely and wanted to be with her sisters again. These saints had sacrificed their one chance at life for some specious idea of holiness, and we were supposed to admire their halos. We were supposed to want to be like them.

Studying the lives of saints was a conspiracy to hold us back from a full life, forcing us to always postpone joy for a tomorrow that might or might not come. It stunted our freedom to be whoever we wanted to be. It caged us.

Before his descent into illness-induced-piety, Felipe had lived. Felipe had taken big, greedy gulps of life. He had indulged his inner fatalist. We were all going to die someday, maybe tomorrow, so he lived life to the fullest while he had the chance.

Amalia was wrong. Joaquín had been wrong. I had been very, very wrong. And now it was too late. It was too late to grab Felipe by the hand again and ask him to teach me how to live, to show me how to love freedom.

And blessed John Paul II could rot, for all I cared. He was doing nothing for Felipe.

~ ~ ~

Two years after Joaquín died, we were at his gravesite celebrating his birthday with Ángeles and a couple of her kids. The grave had the prayer card image of the two Joaquín's etched in stone. The artist hadn't quite gotten the heads right, so they were strangely shrunken in relation to their bodies. But Ángeles, especially, would always gush about the engraving, about how handsome her Joaquín looked, how right their decision was to pay extra for this pricey etching. That way, everyone who passed it would know how good a man she'd had.

Felipe reached for my hand at the grave. I thought nothing of it. Sometimes he needed to hold onto me for physical support. But this time, he caressed my hand with his thumb and reached in to whisper something to me.

"Thank you for not leaving me," he said. "Thank you for not giving up on me. You were the only one who always stuck by me."

I didn't know what to say. I felt guilty for all the times in the past that I had vowed in my head to leave him. For all the times that I had silently condemned him to Hell. For all the times I'd vowed to get over him, even if I would not physically leave him.

"And if you ever put such an ugly image of me on my tombstone, I will haunt you for the rest of your life," he added, laughing quietly. "That shit is awful!"

⁓⁓⁓

Toward the end of his fourth year with cancer, Felipe woke up one night and nudged me frantically.

"Look, Ruth! Look over there, in the corner of the room. Do you see it?"

I saw nothing.

"Do you see him? Look! There he is! He's calling me," Felipe said, only then putting on his glasses.

"Who?" I was rubbing my eyes, but I still saw nothing.

"The pope, John Paul! He's calling me. He's telling me to go with him," he said excitedly.

I was stunned. "Don't listen to him," I said sharply. "He isn't real. You're having a nightmare."

Felipe's prayers to the pope grew more fervent in the week that followed. He told the kids about his visit from John Paul, and they'd look at me, wondering if their father had finally lost his marbles.

I dusted the night table and deliberately put the prayer cards under all the junk in the drawer, hoping Felipe's short-term memory problems would make him forget he'd had them. No dice. As soon as the sun went down, he was franticly looking for the cards.

"Have you seen them? They were right here last night?" he said, rummaging under the bed, looking through his clothes drawers.

Finally, I couldn't stand it anymore and I fished them out of the drawer, then flung them at him. "They're getting old and ragged," I said. "I figured we didn't need them anymore."

He just stared at me, saying nothing. That night, he didn't invite me to pray the rosary with him, so I don't know if he just skipped it or did it without me.

Something woke me out of my sleep. It wasn't a loud sound. It was more like a sigh and then a rustle. Felipe was asleep next to me, so I just rolled over and went back to sleep. In the morning, Felipe would not wake up, even after I shoved him violently.

I called his doctor. The EMTs came. The kids arrived right on their tail. His doctor suspected a stroke. The ambulance took him away, two of the kids followed, and one of them waited in the kitchen for me while I got dressed. When I lifted the bed skirt in search of my shoes, I saw what it was I had heard in the night: the pope's prayer card had fallen and the sound of the lamination hitting the wood had awakened me. Joaquín's card was still propped behind the bottle of holy water.

I sat by his bed at the hospital day and night, awaiting his last words, hoping for instructions. They never came. At night, I'd fall asleep on the chair in the room and dream of the pope, or Joaquín, sneaking into my house and getting Felipe to go out to play with them, like naughty children. They'd all giggle on their way out of the room. Felipe slipped away a week later. He never regained consciousness.

Everyone kept reminding me that he was in a better place now, that he had suffered a lot those past four years. They pretended to forget the nonsense that had preceded his disease: the drunken outbursts, the promiscuity, the idiocy that everyone had witnessed. The behavior that had shamed me to my core and had made me feel like a failure. Felipe had died, and with that so had his sins. He had become, they'd intimate, such a good man. And then I became the wife of such a good man, and they'd gush that I had been a saint taking such wonderful care of him during that terrible time, that it must have been so hard for me and that I must be at peace now.

I didn't know how to tell them that they were all so wrong. I had not been a saint. I had been selfish and had realized only when I had him trapped in a cage that Felipe's main ambition in life had been freedom, and without it, life was boring and taxing to him.

Felipe had started to die years ago when cancer had clipped his wings, and I had kept him caged so that I could save him. But he hadn't needed saving. I did. And now I was lost. How to begin to live anew when I had been reading the wrong instruction manual, and the right one had just been buried in a fresh grave?

With his death, his sins were absolved, and he was made new in the collective consciousness. No one went so far as to call him a saint. There were no haloes shadowed onto his pictures. But no one had one bad word to say about him. Not one.

∾ ∾ ∾

When I cleaned out Felipe's clothes months after his death, I also threw away the prayer cards. I threw away my rosary. It would be childish to say that I was mad at God. I wasn't. God and the quest for goodness and beatification just became unimportant. Foolish. Simple. I was going to die, too. I had wasted too much time fighting life, studying the lives of saints, wishing for change in Felipe so that we, together, could walk in the valley of the shadow of death and face no evil. What I had forgotten to do was walk in the valley of the light of life and embrace it in all its flaws and glories.

The kids chalked the change in me up to grief. Henry would invite me over to dinner and to watch fantasy movies with his family. Amalia would invite me to museums, where we'd inevitably end up looking at religious-themed paintings. Eddie would invite me to church on Sundays, even though he didn't drag his own family there. I'd turn him down, making a joke that I had done enough praying for a lifetime with Felipe in his last years.

On Felipe's night table, I had put a framed copy of my favorite picture of him. In it, he's doing a handstand on the old trunk in the backyard. The snow is packed all around him and burdening the branches above. His favorite shearling-lined suede jacket has ridden up his torso, exposing his navel in the cold. The kids are jumping with glee around him. He's smiling his huge, devil-may-care smile.

I hadn't stopped praying. I had just changed the audience. Day and night I now asked that picture of Felipe to send me a sign when he could. No rush—get where you're going—but send me a sign that he'd made it and was happy, that he forgave me. Every day, my prayers would go unanswered.

Until they weren't.

I was sitting on the window seat, reading a fat novel when I saw him. He looked familiar, and his brown suede jacket, also familiar, seemed too warm for the sun that was breaking through the fog. That's what first caught my eye. He was standing still, facing the house but looking down. The wind blew, ruffling the hair around his ears that was peeking out of his cap. He lifted his arm, took off his hat and turned his face up to the sky. It was at that moment that the glory appeared around his head, little tints of rainbow at its edges. We made eye contact. He flashed me a million-megawatt smile, laughed and waved.

I froze for a long second, then nearly broke my neck flying down the stairs to the front door to go to him. I wanted to cry out and chase him, but by the time I got there, it was too late. He was gone.

# LAS TRES MARÍAS

They were following their mother's orders to get out there, explore their new world and make some friends. The three of them walked in the midday sun on the newly laid sidewalks, past streets and streets of brand-new houses that still smelled of fresh cement, right next to construction sites with rebar poking up from dirt and bricks and men hoisting plastic buckets and spraying water from hoses.

"*¡Psssssssst!*" the men would call out. "*¡Psssssssst! ¡Mamitas! ¡Qué liiiindaaas!*"

Their voices would drop at the end, becoming almost a growl. All movement would stop, buckets frozen in mid-air, hoses limply dripping water. The men stared, smiling, some holding their junk.

Their mother had given them explicit instructions on how to deal with such situations: "Don't look up. Never look up. Pretend you don't hear them. Don't give them any importance. Don't give them any hope. Be dignified."

But, as usual, Lola couldn't help herself. Flanked by her sisters, she tilted her face so her downcast eyes could see the men, could see what they were up against. Marisol squeezed her forearm, hard.

The workers, like animals ready to pounce, saw her eyes move to them and jubilated with whistles and choruses of "*¡Uuuyyyy, mamiiiiiitas!*"

Chastened by Marisol's grip on one arm and feeling Pilar's stiff fear on the other side, Lola turned her face away to the street, dramatically rejecting the men. That just made them laugh more, their cackles punctuated by wolf whistles.

One of them called out, "*Las tres Marías, tres corazones, ¡La que va en centro no lleva calzones!*"

Whenever three women stood side by side, someone would inevitably singsong the rhyme, often leading to a jostling on the part of the women to not be the one in the middle, the vulgar one who didn't wear panties. But the playground taunt was wasted on these girls as they couldn't understand it. And the men didn't get to see them jostle.

"What the heck, Lola? What an idiot. You're not supposed to look. You know that!" Marisol scolded her the second they cleared the construction site. "They'll think you're interested. That you like them or something."

"I didn't look! I just peeked," Lola said.

Pilar was crying. Again.

"And stop crying, Pilar," Marisol scolded. "They're not going to do anything to you. They'll get fired."

"How do you know?" Pilar said, mucus dripping from her nose.

"You two are idiots," Marisol kept saying.

The sidewalks were bare of neighbors in the heat of the day, save for the lady across the street sweeping in the shade of her carport. She was quietly chuckling at the scene, laughing at the girls, even if she couldn't understand their bickering. She'd seen them before. "*Las gringas.*" They were new. The boys, including her son, were all a twitter about them. "*Tontas.*"

The Arce girls were each born almost exactly twelve months apart. They so resembled each other that people took them for triplets. Maybe one had more freckles, the other more waves in her hair and the other a little more flesh on her thighs, but to the unfamiliar, they were identical. Marisol was the oldest, followed by Pilar, then Lola. They were always together, sometimes walking around the neighborhood three abreast or sitting on the low carport wall in front of their house, watching their new world go by. Everyone had seen them, taken note of them.

The Arce girls were barely teenagers when they were labeled *gringas*, summarily accused of all the moral lapses attributed by Latinos to every single American woman. They were doomed to become sluts. It was only a matter of time. But they had no idea.

Before they became *gringas* they were just the Arce girls: three suburban sisters, and truly *tres Marías*: María Soledad, María Pilar and María Dolores. They dressed alike until middle school, and after that, their similar outfits at least were in different colors. Their mother took obvious pride in their beauty.

Their first world had been the Boston suburbs of neat Cape Cod houses with tidy lawns, bicycles and hippity-hops strewn overnight in driveways. Their social circle had enjoyed pizza parties, bowling and roller skating. It was a comfortable, happy life.

But when the American Dream ran afoul of double-digit inflation and factory closings in 1981, their parents, María del Carmen and her husband César, pulled up stakes and made a tactical retreat to the Costa Rica they had left in the 1960s, hoping to ride out the uncertain times and stretch their modest dollar savings to buttress more meager wages.

They bought a little house in an unfinished subdivision some four miles outside of downtown San José. It was called Urbanización Florestal, but the name was aspirational. The brand-new subdivision was devoid of mature trees, and saplings were staked like sentinels around the perimeter of a large patchy grass field that, it was hoped, would someday become the leafy central park plaza of the neighborhood.

The Arce family arrived in August, the girls wearing polyester pant suits—maroon for Marisol, sky blue for Lola, soft green for Pilar. They hauled more than a dozen suitcases out of the various cars of family and friends who had gone to greet them at the airport, while a small group of nosy neighbors stood around to wave their welcomes. There were lots of mute smiles and heads nodding toward the English-only speaking daughters of the newly returned couple. They were an oddity, and people were curious.

Hours later, after the girls had fished out their prized skin-tight designer jeans and laid on their beds to work the zippers up—Calvin Klein for Marisol, Sergio Valente for Pilar and Jordache for Lola—they headed out to sit on the cement wall to survey their new neighborhood. By then, the well-wishers were gone, and the streets were practically empty. The only people out were some teenage boys on a park bench, gawking in their direction and apparently too shy to go over to meet the girls.

The *gringas* had landed.

The boys on the bench eventually overcame their reticence. With each passing day, they would get more and more relaxed and, some weeks later, after Lola had lifted her head and nodded at them, they finally made their approach. The group of five boys walked up to the girls and introduced themselves. There was only one who spoke enough schoolbook English to start the conversation.

"Welcome to Costa Rica," he said. "My name is Aurelio."

He introduced his friends, Lucho, Daniel, Pachico and his kid brother, Raúl. Aurelio pointed at the laggards on the bench and rambled off more names. All boys. Boys with whispers of moustaches and chin hairs. The girls were pleased, flattered even. At thirteen, fourteen and fifteen, they glowed in the promise of attention from the teenagers of the opposite sex. Their future in that new neighborhood, they decided that afternoon, looked rosy.

Marisol had started flirting with the upperclassmen in the school hallways back in the States and had left behind two broken-hearted teenagers when her family departed. Pilar was shy and, although she knew she made the middle-school boys tongue-tied, it was a wasted power because she was too tongue-tied herself to put it to use. Lola, at thirteen, was not that into real boys her age yet. A precocious reader, she had read too many Harlequin romances and thought herself ready for the sort of dramatic love affair that seventh-grade boys were incapable of providing.

"Oh my God! Listen to this," she pleaded with her sisters as she read breathlessly from her bed that night, like she did many nights, "'She didn't need to tell him how much she needed his touch. He felt the heat rising off her, came around the sofa and, with one movement, caught her slender waist in the crook of his arm, and his other hand cupped her nape and pulled her, hard, to his mouth. Their bodies were soft against each other, yet hard. . . .'"

"Stop! It's getting nasty," Pilar shrieked, laughing.

Pilar would always shrink and blush at the steamy passages her sister would read aloud from her bed at night, while Marisol would laugh out loud. She had kissed a boy, Marisol would constantly remind her sisters.

"Go to sleep, Lola," Marisol laughed. "In real life, it's nothing like the books."

∾ ∾ ∾

*1992*

*My dearest,*

*No one really knows me. And that's okay. Don't feel bad, I want it that way. You won't know me well, either, but I'll want you to love the me you think you see. What I don't want is for you to ever hear the gossip. I want you to hear the truth from me. I want you to let me tell you what happened.*

*The first time it happened, I had no idea. I thought he wanted to kiss me. I thought we were going to make out. He had picked me up in his car. It was his father's, he said. And he drove me to the empty lot, where the plots of land were just starting to get subdivided and marked. He did kiss me, for a second or two. Then he grabbed my head at its nape and pushed my face down into his crotch. His dick was out of his pants. I had never seen one before. I barely saw it because it was so close to my face, and I tried to pull away. But his grip was strong, and I couldn't lift my face.*

∾ ∾ ∾

After Aurelio and the boys befriended the Arce girls, a routine developed. Having arrived mid-school year, the girls audited classes with the sole goal of learning Spanish in time to be promoted to the next grade by the new academic year. After school, they'd meet up with the boys at the Arce carport on their bikes, and the boys would give the girls tours of Florestal and the surrounding town. Carmen would send them on errands to the butcher or the market, and the boys would tag along, helping the girls carry the bags back on their handlebars. Carmen and César were pleased at the progression of their daughters' language skills through this full immersion experience.

The construction workers didn't bother the girls when the boys were around. And Lola could glare at them with impunity. Otherwise. the workers would make lewd comments and gestures, always introduced with a "*Pssst*."

"Do they think we're going to like them because they *pssst* at us?" Lola asked her father at dinner one night. "Do any of the ladies go and give them their number when they call at them like that?"

"Ha! Hope springs eternal for some men! You'd be surprised at how many girls fall for the catcalls," César laughed, winking.

"That can't be true, Dad," Marisol said. "They're gross."

"No, you're right," he quickly corrected. "They're just stupid guys being guys."

"Guys being guys? You're a guy. Do you do that?" Marisol's mouth twisted in disgust, challenging her father.

"Come on! Of course, not. I'm decent." César looked to Carmen, who just sat there smiling, enjoying the exchange.

"So, it's not just a guy thing, is it? It would be like saying that girls who wave at the catcallers are just being girls, then," Marisol said.

César looked exasperated. "Fine, Marisol. They're not 'just guys.' They're low-class pigs, *pachucos*," César said, then added with a smile, "But, you know, there is a nice way to let girls and women know they look good. Women like to be noticed, just not the way those guys do it. It's called a *piropo*, you know, a nice complement. *Piropos* can be done tastefully."

"I don't know, Dad. I sure don't need strangers commenting on my looks," Marisol said. "I'd bet most girls I know wouldn't."

"If I thought the guy was cute, Marisol, I wouldn't mind," Lola said. "But not those construction workers! When I look at them, it's not to thank them for noticing me. I just want to tell them they're stupid."

"Don't!" said Pilar. "Don't talk to them at all. Mom, we always have to keep Lola from looking at them."

"Lola! Don't be dumb. Ignore them, like I said. Don't ever look at them," Carmen repeated emphatically.

"Mom! I do not look at them all the time. Pilar's exaggerating," said Lola, shooting her sister a hairy eyeball. "But one of these days I am going to tell them off."

César's voice got serious. "Lola, don't talk to them. Don't look at them. They're *pachucos*."

The dinner discussion about catcalling, not the first, not the last, would highlight male-female interaction in the girls' new culture, where men were expected to pull, women to push away. It was a delicate dance. Showing too much attention to boys and men might mark a woman as loose or frivolous. But by twenty-one, most girls of that time aspired to be headed to the altar or already ensconced in their husband's house. If a girl was too picky, she might risk becoming an old maid in her late twenties. And men? They also married young, but it was fairly common for the successful ones (and even the not so successful) to have girlfriends on the side as proof of their virility. Their wives would very often be expected to just endure these extramarital relationships.

It was hard for César and Carmen to teach their daughters the rhythm of that old-fashioned dance because they themselves had become enlightened, Americanized even, in the wake of the sexual revolution they had experienced after they had arrived in the United States. Even with Marisol pointing out the many contradictions, her parents felt it their duty to instruct their daughters on the local customs so that the girls would thrive in Costa Rica. As a result, the tightrope they made the girls walk was simple and straightforward: Always keep your guard up and your eyes down. Although they were finding it was hard to teach subordination to girls who had a sense that they were equal to boys, they repeated their lessons like a scratched record: "Don't encourage the boys and, above all, guard your reputations."

César and Carmen were accustomed in their Boston suburban world to the girls being considered "exceptional" or "interesting" in a way that hid the discomfort people felt when they couldn't put them neatly into a box: were they Americans, foreigners or what? But in Costa Rica, there was no question that they were seen as *gringas*. Because the Arce girls didn't grasp the negative and lasting ramifications of this and instead delighted in their new "otherness" that attracted boys, the girls did not realize that their behavior could be misconstrued as looseness. Maybe their daughters' shorts *were* too short, Carmen and César would whisper to each other, or their self-confidence too brash, or their persistence in speaking with boys too morally lax for the new country. But their parents also feared that speaking too openly about these things, offering too much information about adolescent sexual appetites, would incite the girls to rebel or inspire experimentation. So, they condensed and simplified the warnings. "Watch out," they'd say. "Men are dangerous."

In contrast to Marisol's cool regalness and Lola's feistiness, those warnings would terrify Pilar, who was already inclined to fear the unknown. She would go stiff with anxiety and nudge her sisters almost hysterically if they were caught alone near the catcalling construction workers or sharing the sidewalk with laborers or even in the shop of the gruff-sounding butcher with his bloody coat and lazy eye.

"So, they're not just men. They're something else . . . aberrations, pigs, *pachucos*," continued Marisol, who wasn't about to let her father off the hook for his initial comments about catcallers. "So, all men are NOT created equal . . ."

"Don't be a smart aleck, Marisol, and don't put words into my mouth," César said, annoyed. "I'm just saying, don't pay attention to *pachucadas*, those rude and crass comments. Listen to your mother and just ignore them. Don't look at them. Don't talk to them. Don't give them the satisfaction of your reaction."

"Here's what I don't get," Marisol continued, obviously having ignored César's comments. "If these guys, the ones who think we're asking for it by wearing shorts or flipping our hair or just having been born pretty, aren't regular guys, good guys like you or our friends, why don't you guys go up and tell them to lay off, that they're pigs, that the next time you hear one of them hiss a *pssst* or a *mamita* or a *qué ricas* tossed at some girl, you're going to kick their asses. Why does everyone in this country just accept this as the way things are?"

César had no response, but Carmen stood up, casually started picking up the dishes and answered her. "Because violence solves nothing, Marisol. Some people, lowlifes don't want to learn and will never learn. You can't change everything. This is just the way things are here," she said. "This is a *machista* country. Some guys would proposition a three-legged dog if they saw she was female, because they think they have to compliment all girls in order to prove their manliness."

"So let me get this straight," said Lola, enjoying the opportunity to join her older sister in challenging her parents, "if some guy hollers *¡Adiós!* to me, and I think he's cute, it's okay not to ignore him, and I can wave and smile at him and encourage him . . ."

"But only if he's not a lowlife," interjected Marisol, drolly. "The problem isn't all men, you're saying, just disgusting men. But it's not their problem. It's our problem. We girls are the ones who have to figure out who is who, pretending we don't understand that the gross ones are treating us like caged animals because good, virtuous, ignorant girls who are worthy of landing husbands don't notice those sorts of things. They're dignified. See how ridiculous this can get?"

"Oh, for real! Don't make a federal case about this. You're just being argumentative. You're no dummies," Carmen shot back. "You'll know instinctively when guys are up to no good and when men are decent like your father."

"But will we really, Mom?" Marisol asked.

Lola, smiling, nudged her with her elbow in solidarity. Pilar had checked out of the conversation way earlier, but looked up at that question, as if expecting a clarifying answer.

Carmen rolled her eyes at her daughters. "Don't go too overboard with this feminism stuff, Marisol. Guys are put off by that."

"Raúl told me that," said Lola, nodding earnestly at her sister. "He said guys are turned off by girls who think they're more powerful or better than them. No offense, Marisol, but he said a lot of the guys think you're too stuck up."

"Oh, yeah, Raúl should know," Marisol said, rolling her eyes. "I'll try to remember to bat my eyelashes more next time we see them all. I'll try to remember not to overreact."

It was only a few days later when Lola overreacted. Walking in front of an almost-finished house some three blocks from theirs, one of the workers let go a lecherous growl before calling at them with a *pssst*. Another worker wolf-whistled.

Lola stopped abruptly, turned to them defiantly with her hands on her hips and said in her accented Spanish, "Did you lose your cat?"

Instead of recoiling with shame and apologetically getting back to their jobs, the men became feral. "*¡Uuuuuy, mamitas! ¡Qué ricas!*"

They laughed and growled, letting loose a string of vulgar catcalls punctuated by the word "*gringas*" and whistles. Two of the workers came to the edge of the sidewalk, blocked the girls' path and reached out to touch them. The three sisters froze in terror. Even Lola, who had thought she was only up against words, was scared. From across the street, an older woman came out wielding her broom and scolding the men. She crossed the street and started whacking them with the broom. They quickly moved away, laughing and returned to their jobs. The girls scurried away, their hearts beating fast.

"See, Lola, see!" Pilar kept repeating, scolding, practically shrieking, "I told you so. We told you so."

The woman scolded them, too. "*¡Tontitas!*" she called them.

Chastened, Lola stopped trying to stare down the construction workers or dream about challenging them. But she continued to complain about them all the time. The sisters' male friends would only shrug and say nothing. These boys, too, had fantasized about running their hands along the girls' bodies. They harbored hopes that the rumors about *gringas* were true. They were ready if the girls were.

∾ ∾ ∾

*I started to cry. Of course. He made soothing sounds: "Shhshhshhshh. Don't cry," he said. "This is special. This will make you special to me. Just kiss it a little." I wanted to run away, but I kissed it so he would let go. "No," he said. "Not like that. Kiss it with your mouth open. With your tongue, like I taught you how to kiss." Then he shoved his dick in my mouth, and I couldn't cry anymore. But I heard the voices. There were people coming, they were riding bikes and laughing. I squirmed, desperate to stop, to not be seen. "Shhshhshhh," he said. "Don't get up. Stay there. If they see you, they'll think you're a slut. You'll get a bad reputation."*

∾∾∾

It wasn't until the semester ended in December that the Arce girls made girlfriends. In their initial months, it had seemed that there were no girls their ages in the new neighborhood. They'd sit on the cement wall of the carport, often surrounded by a group of local boys, practicing their conversational Spanish and generally enjoying the attention. The girls they met at school didn't live in the neighborhood and didn't invite them over to their homes. When they did start noticing other girls, at the *pulpería* or standing in line to use the payphone on the far end of the park, they were greeted with cold shoulders, the girls looking at their feet, pretending not to notice them, ignoring them.

They thought it odd, but they had each other, so it didn't matter too much. Once summer vacation hit, however, some of the boys who had gotten to know the Arce girls brought other girls around to meet them. Daniel introduced them to his sister, Vanessa, a fifteen-year-old with green eyes. Then Aurelio and Raúl's neighbor, Laura, came over with him one afternoon and introduced herself, her bookish thick glasses and unattractive features matching a jarring cackle she let loose at the slightest provocation. And Pachico brought his cousin, who lived around the block from him: the athletic Úrsula, who showed up wearing running shorts and carrying a volleyball. She invited the sisters to play in the park.

It became the summer of volleyball. Someone in the group procured a net that they staked into the parched park ground. Every day they played, co-ed teams picked on the spot, depending on the mood. More boys joined in, their bikes strewn at the edge of the field. The Arce girls reveled in their new, cute sporty selves, borrowing César's sweatbands and wristbands to complete their outfits. Úrsula outplayed everyone, but the other girls were nothing if not energetic. The boys, at first distracted by the flesh and sweat of the girls, soon became competitive and made sure they appeared stronger and better than the girls. The boys often interrupted the games to "teach" the girls better form, standing behind an Arce girl and manipulating her arms into place, sometimes touching her waists to emphasize their point.

They would all break for lunch, then find their way back to the park in the late afternoon, when it was cooler. The group grew. More and more, as evening fell, they'd find their way to the Arce carport, where the Arce sisters and their three girlfriends would soon be surrounded by double the number of boys.

The Arce sisters were incredibly happy. They felt free, and the most urgent thing in their new life was to have fun. They thought it perfect. In bed at night, they'd catch up on the day's events in the dark. Lola would often end the conversation by squealing, "Pinch me! This is a dream. A utopia." Marisol would laugh and add, "Another day in paradise." Pilar would smile.

Their mother would spend the day sewing and then deliver her products in the late afternoon. Upon returning home, she would call the girls in to help prepare the evening meal. The other girls, in turn, would go home to help their own mothers cook. The boys would scatter. After dinner, in the cool night air, they'd all gravitate back to the carport.

César, who worked two jobs to keep them afloat, would roll in at around 8:30 and have to honk at the boys who were blocking the entrance to the carport. They'd make way, just enough for his car to pass and then fill in the space again.

At the beginning of summer, César and Carmen took it all in stride. They'd greet the gang and sometimes stay and engage in conversation. But the relentlessness of it started to take its toll around January.

"Girls," César began somberly on an unusually lonely Sunday evening, "you cannot keep hanging outside with a gazillion guys every night. It doesn't look right."

"People are going to start talking," Carmen supported her husband.

The girls started speaking all at once: "That's stupid!" "You say, don't worry about what people say!" "They're our friends!" "We play SPORTS with them, DAD!"

César continued cautiously, serving himself salad as he spoke and not looking at them. "Those boys, a lot of them are *pachuquillos* . . . I think."

"DAD!" the girls shrieked in unison, aghast at the accusation.

"No, they're not lowlifes, Dad. They don't have much money . . . In case you haven't noticed, not everyone here is rich like us Americans," Marisol said, her voice oozing contempt.

"Hey, watch it!" César warned but then laughed and said, "If you think we're rich, I've got a bridge to sell you! We're definitely not rich, but we're not low-class either. Your mom and I want to make sure we keep it that way."

After that night, when César would roll in and the crowd was large, he stopped greeting them. He'd just glare at the boys. Sometimes he'd say, "Enough," which meant they had to leave. Sometimes, tired, he'd ignore them and slam the front door behind him. Then Carmen would come out a minute later, looking tense, and order the girls in.

Despite the vigilance of their parents, it was inevitable that love would come to the Arce girls. First off, Marisol and Aurelio became a couple. He was smart and handsome, wore Lacoste shirts and Puma sneakers and went to a boys' private school. They'd talk about President Reagan's dangerous interest in the region, the tragic civil war in El Salvador and what books they were reading, all of which led to a meeting of minds and souls . . . and waist-up make outs.

Lola latched onto to her hopelessly romantic kindred spirit, Raúl. Together they'd spend hours with their ears stuck to a boombox playing, rewinding and re-playing love ballads in English and Spanish in order to get every lyric down in a little yellow notebook they shared. Despite her encyclopedic knowledge of Harlequin storylines, she and Raúl were in puppy love, holding hands and giving each other little kisses and soft embraces.

Pilar flitted around. One week she crushed on one boy, then next week on another. She always seemed vaguely disinterested but sometimes let them drape their arms around her shoulders and kiss her. Mostly, she let them just bask in her beauty. Until Freddy rolled in.

Freddy was nobody's friend, really. Some of the guys knew him or of him, but he did not attend any of their schools. In fact, none of them seemed too fond of him. At 5'10", he was the tallest of all the boys and his pecs were always nicely on display beneath his fitted T-shirts. His curly dark hair was on the shaggy side, but the way he'd use his hand to push his bangs out of his sparkling blue eyes when he laughed gave him a movie-star quality. And yet, despite his good looks, he always seemed out of place in the group.

Freddy had come over to one of the pickup volleyball games in mid-January and, like the other boys, he ended up at the carport. He hung out on the periphery, staring at Pilar.

"That Freddy guy is staring at Pilar," Pachico said to Marisol one evening. "I don't know about him."

"Pachico," she said sternly, "no one likes jealous guys."

In truth, the girls loved it when the boys would get jealous of their conversations with other boys or imagined looks or flirtations. The boys' jealousy read like love to them. They'd sigh about it with pretend exasperation in their bedtime chats.

A few days later, Freddy moved in from the periphery and sidled up to Pilar. As the evening progressed, he and Pilar could be seen with their heads close to each other, speaking in whispers that no one else could hear. He was playing *hormiguita* on her arm, caressing it in little ant steps, then randomly pinching her skin like an ant bite. Every time the ant would bite, Pilar would let out a little shriek and giggle. He would beam and chuckle, and the game would go on.

When César would roll up, Freddy would step away from the group and make himself scarce. It took only a few days for César to notice him, though, and rather than going inside and slamming the door, he lingered until Freddy looked up and they locked eyes. For a long second, there was recognition, as if César knew him.

César uttered, "Shhhhhhoo!" as if scaring a cat away.

Freddy tipped his imaginary cap and walked away.

～～～

*"That was good," he said afterward. "You're learn-*
*ing." I was so embarrased. Incredibly embarrassed. I*
*couldn't look at him. He dropped me off at the bus stop.*
*I jumped out of the car, praying nobody had seen me in*
*it. When I didn't say anything before closing the door,*
*he reached over, rolled down the window and said, I'll*
*see you next week." I wasn't so sure I wanted to.*

∾∾∾

When summer vacation ended at the beginning of February, there was a détente in the Arce household. The girls were straight-A students. After a semester of language catch-up and a summer of fun with the locals, they were put in a bilingual private school that stretched the budget but satisfied their need for intellectual stimulation. Homework also kept the boys away most nights, with the exception of Aurelio, who would come to do homework with Marisol, and the girlfriends, who came and went as they pleased. Every few nights, César would come home after work and report that he had seen Freddy and some other guy sitting on the bench out in front of the carport. Marisol and Lola would shrug. Pilar would blush. It wasn't lost on Carmen. She saw it.

One Saturday morning, mother and daughters were walking across to the taxi stand, when one of the local ladies greeted them, singing *"Las tres Marías, tres corazones . . ."* and the woman's teenage daughter standing within earshot added the refrain, *". . . la que va en el centro es una putilla."*

Pilar, standing in the middle, was the whore mentioned in the song, and hung her head down. Carmen stiffened but did not wipe the smile from her face, just continued walking. When they were past the women, Carmen faced her daughters calmly and said, "You're getting a bad reputation. This is what your father and I were warning you about. You have to be better than everyone else, or they'll think you're typical *gringas*. They'll think you let those boys touch you, and worse. . . . You cannot let them think that."

"Mom, Aurelio says it's too late," Marisol dared to answer. "He says that the reason only Vanessa and Laura are allowed to hang out with us is because their parents studied in the States. He also said Úrsula is a *marimacha*, so her rules are different. All the girls in the neighborhood decided we were sluts from the minute we landed. That's what their mothers told them. And they're not allowed to be seen with us."

Lola was outraged. "I can't believe you never told us that, Marisol! What the heck? I've been super nice to all these stupid girls, trying to be friends with them," she said. "I'm never talking to them again. I don't care if they don't like me. I don't like them. I never want to like them."

"Don't be so hasty," Carmen said. "Sometimes you need to let people get to know you better so that they can see the real you. You can't let them go on thinking you're a bad girl just because they're ignorant. Show them who you are."

"Forget it, Mom. Lola's right," said Marisol. "Who cares what they think! They're small minded. And bigoted. I don't know them, and I don't like them, already. I have zero interest in being their friend."

"But if you insist on hanging out with so many guys, they're going to think they're right, that you're just sluts," Carmen insisted.

"Girls and guys can be friends, Mom. The world is changing," said Lola.

"Mom, this goes back to the whole 'keep your eyes down' theory with catcallers," Marisol began again. "Girls can't win here! We're not supposed to be too friendly with guys, and if we are, we're floozies. But somehow, we're supposed to find a guy. We're not supposed to respond to catcallers, but if we ignore them, the guys start calling us stuck up, and if we complain, we're too sensitive. One more thing: Girls here are not equal, and no one seems to care. Not even the girls!"

"I'll agree with you that it can seem confusing sometimes," Carmen answered. "But it's not as hard as you make it out to be. You just have to be smart about these things. And it doesn't matter how rational your arguments are or how good you think you are. If you get a bad reputation, that's all people will see you for."

The conversation went back and forth like that for a while. It was so animated that none of them noticed that Pilar had not said a word but looked like she was about to cry.

"What happened to you?" Lola snapped when she noticed her sister's crumbling face. "Who cares what she called you. You know you're not a slut."

Pilar said nothing.

Carmen noticed, and in the following weeks, kept her ears open, talking to the neighbor women over their backyard walls while they hung out the laundry or were waiting in line at the market or for the payphone. She gained their confidence, earned their friendship and invited gossip. She tried bringing up Freddy because her mother's intuition after peeking at her daughter and him snuggling close on the wall, and then César reporting him sitting nearby after he'd been banished, and how Pilar would look away if ever his name was mentioned made her think something was amiss. But at the mention of his name, lips became sealed and the conversations ended abruptly.

Pilar continued to maintain her silence.

∾ ∾ ∾

*He said he would tell my sisters about us, so that they could talk some sense into me. He said he owed me an apology, and he wanted to do it in person. So, I agreed to see him again. My new school friend, Adriana, let us meet at her house. He was her cousin. She pretended she had somewhere to be and left as soon as we got into her house. He was in the den on the couch. The TV was showing some strange Japanese cartoon. He patted the seat next to him, inviting me to sit there. He didn't lie. He did apologize to me. He said he was sorry he had gone so fast. He said it was my fault because I was so pretty. He said he just couldn't control himself. He started making out with me, and the next thing I knew, we were laying down and he was sort of on top of me. He pulled my shirt over my head and when it got stuck on one arm, I struggled to get out of there. He said, "Shshshshsh, don't worry, I won't hurt you." "I don't think this is right," I said. "Shshshshsh," he said while taking off my pants. I could hear the rain coming down on the tin roof. He laughed when he saw my panties. "Those are grandma panties!" he said. I was cold. I was shivering. He didn't bother taking off my grandma panties. He just moved them over.*

∾ ∾ ∾

It was Lola who finally spoke up. She and Raúl were sitting on the carport wall one rare, non-rainy afternoon, picking out the lyrics to Marty Balin's *Hearts* and discussing the merits of true heartbreak.

"You know your sister Pilar is heartbroken," Raúl said.

"Pilar?"

"She and Freddy have been fighting."

"They're not even together," Lola scoffed.

He stared at her for a second. "You didn't know? They write letters to each other every single day. Her classmate, Adriana, is their go-between. Adriana is his cousin. You didn't know?"

For a change, Lola was speechless. Adriana was one of the very few schoolmates that any of them ever hung out with. Pilar had even been to her house a few times.

"Why are they fighting?"

Raúl, looking uncomfortable and realizing too late he had given up a secret, answered, "Everybody knows. How come you don't?"

"What problems are they having?" Lola demanded.

"I can't say."

"You *can't* or you *won't* say?"

"I can't. I don't know how to say it to you."

"Then go away," she said, grabbing her yellow notebook and the boombox and retreating into the house.

Pilar was on her bed, her schoolbooks spread out in front of her. Lola threw a teddy bear at her head, knocking her out of her reverie.

"I heard about you and Freddy," she whispered fiercely. "What the heck, Pilar? Why didn't you tell me?"

Pilar looked stricken and about to cry. Again.

"Don't cry. Tell me!" Lola whispered. "Tell me everything."

Pilar just shook her head and said, "I can't. It has to be over."

"Why? Why does it have to be over?"

"I just can't anymore," said Pilar, tears now flowing.

Seeing that, Lola changed her tone and ran over to hug her sister.

∾ ∾ ∾

*Afterward, I was sitting on the couch, my clothes back on, hugging my legs, crying. Adriana had not come back yet. He was mad at me. "You're a liar!" he said. "You HAVE done this before. I should have known. You're a gringa. Who was it? Which of the guys was it?" I kept repeating that I had never done it before. I said I never wanted to do it again. I said what we did was very wrong. I said it was a sin. I said I wanted to go home. He kept calling me a liar. He said that there hadn't been enough blood. I walked myself to the bus stop before Adriana even came back.*

∽∽∽

"Poor you! Love is so, so hard."

Marisol walked in on this scene. "What's wrong with Pilar?"

"Her heart is broken," Lola said.

"Pachico? Lucho?" Marisol's voice was less concerned than droll.

"Freddy."

Marisol looked alarmed. "Stay away from him, Pilar. None of the guys like him. Aurelio won't tell me why. But stay away from him. He gives me the creeps."

∽∽∽

*He said he would tell my father that I was a slut, that I had been sleeping around with all the boys. He said he wanted to give me a second chance. He said that even though I had betrayed his trust, he'd let me make it up to him. I was afraid my family would find out. I felt dumb. I agreed to go back, even though I really didn't want to. This time, I took off my own clothes. This time, he complimented my pink bikinis.*

99

*This time, he showed no mercy. He was relentless.
This time, the towel that I hadn't notice him set down
on the couch beneath us was covered in blood. The
inside of my thighs was covered in blood. This time, I
bawled. "Shshshshsh, mamita," he said. "Don't cry.
I'm sorry. I was wrong. You weren't lying to me. I was
just too gentle last time. Shshshshsh, I'm not mad at
you anymore."*

∽∽∽

It was late April, and the girls were planning their collective birthday party for mid-June. Pilar would be fifteen and would be celebrated as a *quinceañera*. Marisol, who hadn't wanted a party at fifteen, would celebrate her Sweet Sixteen in the American tradition alongside her. They'd decided on a house party with a DJ spinning records and the cousins and friends dancing. Lola, turning an uneventful fourteen, was going along for the ride with her name on the communal cake.

"Freddy better NOT come to our party," Marisol said to Pilar, "or I'll tell on you."

After school, the girls would finish their homework, move their books aside and get to work coloring in the parchment paper invitations they had decided on for the party. Pilar's curly penmanship invited cousins, friends and neighbors to celebrate their birthdays and the anniversary of their moving to Costa Rica. While Marisol and Lola colored in the sketches of flower baskets on the invitation and discussed the playlist for the DJ, Pilar worked quietly and deliberately, immune to the ruckus.

At the end of May, Carmen took the girls to the fabric shop to pick out a pattern for their party dresses. They'd decided that each one would have a different style and a totally different print, for the first time expressing their individual identities. At home, Carmen took out her notepad and took their measurements, like she did every time she was going to sew them outfits. The notebook held their measurements from many past dresses, like a growth chart on a kitchen doorframe. The girls took turns getting measured in age order. Carmen wrapped the tape measure around Marisol's hips first, jotted down the number, then her waist and finally her breast. She repeated the procedure with Pilar. She stopped and looked at her past notes and re-measured her breast. "Hmmm," she said. She looked at her daughter's face. Pilar looked away, and Carmen just moved on to Lola.

The day of the party, the girls and Carmen and their cousins worked from early morning, cooking and setting up streamers and balloons and re-arranging the furniture to create a dance floor. At 1 o'clock, they went to church for Mass and a blessing that Carmen said they had to have because it was a birthday tradition. Everyone was at church: their friends in suits and dresses, some with bouquets for them, others with little wrapped gifts of chocolates or soaps or perfumes.

The congregation arrived en masse at their house, where the women were working feverishly to keep the food coming while the men hung out in the little backyard, smoking cigarettes and drinking beer. The teenagers immediately started dancing on the improvised space to Michael Jackson, The Police, Bob Marley and El Gran Combo recordings. It was hot and crowded, but delightful.

When the DJ switched to slow numbers, from somewhere in the crowd Freddy materialized and came over to Pilar. She froze, then started shaking her head no. Aurelio saw her, grabbed Marisol, and they approached Freddy.

"You weren't invited," Marisol said curtly. "Leave."

Freddy just smiled and held his hand out to Pilar. She took it and followed him to the dance floor, where they swayed. She stiffly; he pressing too closely.

"Leave," Marisol repeated.

"C'mon, man," said Aurelio. "You heard her. Don't ruin this."

"She wants me here," said Freddy, pulling his head back to look at Pilar and dancing them into the more crowded part of the floor.

Marisol went out back to find her father. They came back together, walking quickly with purpose. Carmen noticed and followed them instinctively.

The three of them pushed through the crowd, and César grabbed Freddy's shoulder.

"Go away, Pilar," he barked at his daughter.

"Get her away from here," Carmen ordered Lola, who had just approached them.

Freddy swept his shoulder with his hand as if brushing off some debris.

"I told you not to come here," César said.

"Your daughters invited me," Freddy said, taking out a cigarette and putting it between his lips.

"No, they didn't. You need to leave," César said, raising his voice and snapping away the cigarette. "And you need to leave right now."

The music was still playing but the couples had moved toward the walls, leaving César and Freddy center stage. César grabbed Freddy's shirt collar in his fists and pulled him close so that, for a split second, they looked to be slow dancing.

Freddy puckered his lips and mimicked kissing César. "Easy, boss, easy, I'm leaving," he uttered impudently.

César's self-restraint held, but before letting go of Freddy's shirt, he hissed, "Listen, you piece of shit, if I ever see you near this house again, I'll fuck you up good," and shoved him away.

❧❧❧

*I don't know why I kept going. I think I didn't know how to not go. How to say no. I know I was afraid my parents would find out. But mostly, I just didn't know how to say no to him. Adriana knew. She barely talked to me anymore. She just would pass his notes to me. We'd go to her house together, and then she'd leave. She would barely look at him. But always, before she left, she'd purse her lips, pierce me with her eyes and silently say, "Slut." I had been wasted. I had nothing more to lose. I WAS a slut. He'd say as much. That I was super easy. That it had taken nothing to convince me because, after all, I was a* gringa. *He said that's why I kept coming back for more. He said that if I ever did this with another boy, I'd be a whore. He was right: I was stuck with him forever. I WAS his. It was too late to change who I was.*

❧❧❧

Freddy put his hands up as if in surrender and walked away toward the front door. Before stepping out, however, he turned around with a huge smile on his face and said, "*Suegro,* the baby is mine."

The horrified gasps of the partygoers were buried by the roar from César, who charged like a bull, dipping his head and running into Freddy's chest with such force that both flew out the open door, over the two steps and onto the carport pavement. César pushed himself up, straddled Freddy and proceeded to punch him over and over and over again in the matter of seconds it took for the other men at the party to reach him and drag him off the boy. Freddy's beautiful face was pulp by then, but despite the crash landing and the assault, he sprung up the minute he was freed from César's weight and put up his fists.

"C'mon, c'mon!" Freddy taunted César.

His arms pinned by his cousins and uncles, César swung his legs, barely making contact with Freddy.

Freddy laughed open-mouth, blood dripping down his teeth, feinting and ducking. Other men intervened and manhandled Freddy out of the carport, ordering him to go away. They picked up rocks and threw them at him, with bad aim, and threatened that they were going to call the cops if he didn't disappear.

No one called the police, and even if they had, they would not have done anything. César's outburst, his violence, shocked no one. They would have expected no less. At some point, they'd also expect him to demand justice for his daughter and a name for his grandchild. He'd shake hands with Freddy and begrudgingly accept him as his son-in-law.

The party ended abruptly. The women and girls were the first to leave. The boys followed, stumbling out, knocking into each other in their hurry to get out the door without being noticed. The DJ stood awkwardly behind his turntables, mute. Most guests were unable to even murmur a goodbye. Pilar had locked herself in the bathroom. Carmen, Marisol and Lola were all crying, huddled at the back of the kitchen. Some cousins lingered to clean up the mess, stopping every so often to rub Carmen's back. No one sought to comfort Pilar.

As the gossip smothered all other neighborhood conversation in the next few days, the relief of other mothers could be felt. Pilar hadn't been the only one. Freddy had been the author of shame in other families in the neighborhood.

But no one had talked about it. His crimes were shrouded in silence. He'd had his way with some of the "good" girls who were assiduous in staying away from the *gringas* for fear of slutty contagion. Mothers had caught their daughters with him in compromising situations. They feared their bad reputations would hold them from other, better prospects later. They feared their daughters being labeled as sluts. Many a mother had failed to see what Freddy was. His pretty baby face belied his age: twenty-one. He was an experienced seducer of naïve teenagers.

The neighborhood boys knew Freddy's age, and they knew he was bad news. They were afraid of him, and of his father, who their fathers had warned had a reputation for picking up whatever was at hand—bottles, rebar scraps—when he'd had one too many (which was just about every night) and make a target of the nearest man, boy or dog.

Freddy's father had set the example two decades earlier, when he fooled the sheltered daughter of a wealthy family into thinking that he had impregnated her. The truth was that he had only forced a kiss onto her unsuspecting lips and shoved his tongue into her mouth but convinced the naïve girl that it was enough to conceive a child. Horrified of the shame she'd bring upon herself and her family, she begged her father to let her marry this lowly son of a barkeep, saying that she loved him. She never told her father about the kiss and only learned the truth after Freddy was conceived, when she experienced a more lasting type of violence. Freddy's father went on to spend the money her family gave her on other women and booze. Her family never asked for her back. They just let her social stature fall a little more with each passing year.

❦ ❦ ❦

*When he exposed me at the party, I never told them what happened. I let them, my sisters, my parents, think I just wanted him. I didn't know how to explain how I kept going back. Why did I keep going back? I didn't think they'd believe me when I said I had been desperate to escape him, but that I had been trapped. My perdition became my cage, and he didn't even have to put a lock to it. I had nowhere to go for salvation. I said nothing for days. I just cried.*

❧❧❧

In the week after the party, the other mothers ignored the drawn drapes at the Arce house and let themselves in to whisper condolences and words of support for Carmen, never leaving without offering to make canapes for the wedding party. Carmen would murmur words of thanks and not let on that there would be no wedding.

Pilar would not be marrying Freddy. While the girls huddled and cried in their bedroom, Carmen and César conferred in the darkness of theirs, hatching a plan to defy convention and to give Pilar a chance to erase the inevitability that was stirring in her womb. They knew they could trust no one. Their family would be aghast at their apostasy, at the desecration of all that was holy—the sanctity of a Costa Rican family—regardless of its provenance or shrouded truths.

Time was not on their side. Not knowing who to turn to, they confided in Marisol and armed her with a tub of coins to go lay siege on the payphone and query her friends back in the States. They tasked her with getting a name, an appointment. They demanded discretion. She complied.

Marisol and Lola were tainted by proximity to Pilar. The boys and the girls stopped coming by the carport. Lola's romantic dreams lost their luster. The one day that Raúl dared stop in to check on her, she handed him the yellow notebook and told him she didn't want it back. She threw the Harlequin romances into the kitchen garbage.

Pilar stayed hidden, which suited Carmen just fine. Although Carmen was resolute in the decision she and César had made for their daughter, it hadn't occurred to her to inform Pilar or even to comfort her. She didn't know how to talk to Pilar, she was so angry. If Pilar had listened to her, them, this would never have happened. And worse, maybe Pilar had lived up to her stereotype; maybe she had been polluted by the American way of thinking even before they had landed in Costa Rica. Too much freedom was bad. There were rules for a reason.

By July, the Arce family had packed up their things and left. There was no triumphant return to the tidy suburbs they had left the year before. Instead, they slunk into the fabric of Hialeah, where Spanish was the lingua franca and where the stories of narrow escapes from the turmoil of Latin America in the early 1980s would obscure the gossip of girls gone wrong. There, the Arce girls would no longer be sluts. There, they'd stop being *gringas*.

Despite this "happy" ending, the girls quietly longed for the early days in Costa Rica before they knew they were doomed to be sluts. They pined for the year when life was about playing volleyball and hanging out with friends and making out under the carport. When Marisol believed that people like her and Aurelio would be the future of the country. When Lola believed that love was as portrayed in romance novels and song lyrics. When Pilar was just a shy middle child before she had been ruined. They longed for that place, that all-too-brief magical place. Their utopia, the place where they had last been children.

≈≈≈

*I had no idea I was going in for an abortion. I thought I was just going to the doctor. I don't think I even knew what an abortion was. I had no idea about anything. But when the doctor made Mom leave the room so that he could talk to me alone, and I saw Mom's face look panic-stricken, begging me with her eyes, I knew everything. I knew this was my chance at redemption. I knew she was trying to save me. And I told the doctor, "Yes. This is my idea. This is what I want."*

≈≈≈

Their house in Urbanización Florestal was abandoned for many months until it sold the following year. By the end of the 1980s, the tourism boom hit Costa Rica and thousands and then, even later, hundreds of thousands of *gringos* descended upon it. But it would take a long time for the Arce girls, *las gringas*, to be forgotten in Urbanización Florestal. They were a legend, a cautionary tale. Their lives became fictionalized. They had slept with ALL the boys, all three of them had taken turns with Freddy, Pilar wasn't the only one who got pregnant, their parents supplied them with birth control pills so the girls could mess around with abandon. The legend took on political and religious dimensions: César and Carmen were communists and they refused to teach their daughters morals. Their fate was what happened when the Church is abandoned.

Even the boys who were closest to them, Aurelio, Raúl, Lucho and Pachico, were tainted. Because of the girls, they, too, had been corrupted by carnal knowledge, and for months thereafter the good girls ignored them. But because they were boys, their bad reputations faded within weeks. And even the girls who had secretly fallen prey to Freddy had their slates wiped clean. Later, no one questioned the white dresses they wore at their weddings.

∽∾∽

*It didn't take long for my sisters to forgive my stupidity. We reinvented ourselves. We went to college. We became successful. People say we are good. They congratulate our parents for having raised such wonderful daughters. We rarely talk about our time in Florestal, but I know we've all thought about it. In many ways, my reinvention was only superficial, like I lived my life in a costume. When I've thought of Freddy over the years, his memory fills me with self-loathing, reminds me of how I allowed myself to be disgraced. When these thoughts roll in, it's as if I'm blinded by Klieg lights. The acting stops, and I'm revealed. I go out into the audience, pick the first good looking guy to hook up with and expose myself as the slut I still feel I am deep inside. I stop pretending I'm innocent. Or good. Their sexual attention validates me, and afterward the sharp edges of the stage lights soften a bit, and I can go on with my act as if there has been no unexpected intermission. My costume, my performance, covers the truth: I was ruined.*

*But now there's you. You're deep inside now. You, I'll keep. You'll also see me in my role. You'll think me successful, good, confident. I'm a good actress; you won't see the shame. Maybe with you I'll finally forget about him. Maybe the playacting will end. Maybe not. Maybe I'll never know what I really am. But I will know this: No matter what happens to you, you will always be a good girl to me.*

*Your mother,*
*Pilar*

# LA FAMILIA

The story was legend in my family. In the beginning, when he was just a bourgeois doctor, Rafael Ángel Calderón Guardia helped my grandmother die.

My grandfather would turn up at his Barrio Escalante house after hours, and the doctor would prattle on and on about how social class didn't matter, that the only difference among men is between those who suffer and those whose duty it is to alleviate that suffering. While he preached, he'd fill the little amber bottle that Abuelito would humbly hand him. Then Calderón Guardia would caution him, as he did every time, to dole out only four drops at a time to be placed under my grandmother's tongue. The good doctor would add that he'd be praying for her, praying for a good death. My grandfather, stone-faced but betraying emotion by the tears forming in his eyes, would nod curtly in thanks and mount his horse for the three-mile ride to his riparian house that smelled of rotting human flesh. There, his wife, the mother of his five children, lay in their bed, dying of the breast cancer that had ulcerated her bosom. Her death took months, and Calderón Guardia's drops were her only solace on that terrible journey.

Later, after the good doctor had become the conservative president, Abuelito cheered at the news reports of his May

Day social guarantees policy, when the man who had eased his wife's death had marched hand-in-hand with the Communist Party leader. There in the stands, lending moral support, was the president's good friend, the monsignor, waving evidentiary papal encyclicals as proof that God approved of their radical ideas. Abuelito was overjoyed that his country, the Church and socialism could marry so that the poor could die less horrible deaths and the workers could have more rights and the children could pray "Ave María" before class started. It made him inordinately proud to be Costa Rican.

Even when rumors started that the good doctor was becoming power hungry, that he was messing with the ballots and that the communists were taking over, Abuelito had his back. He'd hold meetings in the living room, galvanizing his neighbors to rally around him, to pick up arms in his defense, if necessary.

"He's a good man," he'd bellow, pounding his big, meaty hand on the table in the living room.

His daughter-in-law, my mother and the wife of his eldest son, would sneer in the kitchen while she poured out the coffee and plated the *tamal* for her widowed father-in-law and the local politicians in the next room. She'd lean down close to me, her lips brushing my hair and whisper, "*Qué viva Figueres, mi amorcito*." Then she'd wink at me, leave me playing with my toys at the kitchen table and go serve them on a tray painted with purple orchids, the national flower and symbol of the opposition leader, José Luis Figueres Ferrer. Don Pepe, as he was called, the transformer who'd remind folks not to let social reforms get out ahead of local customs, wanted to go beyond bananas and coffee to modernize the country's economy.

If the Church and the communists and the populist leader sharing a bed in a *ménage a trois* was an odd sight, then just as kinky was the next bedroom where the oligarchs—spiteful that Calderón Guardia had actually implemented social reforms instead of just paying lip service to them on Sundays —jumped into bed with the Figuerista band of intellectuals, *nouveau bourgeoisie* and professionals.

The civil war lasted only forty-four days, but Figueres emerged victorious and started his national liberation from ruling elites and oligarchic bedfellows by nationalizing the banks, then abolishing the military and all the while reneging on his promise against reprisals. Calderonistas and communists alike lost their jobs, their properties and some, including their namesake, went into exile.

Abuelito went to Kentucky. We stayed behind.

I was little in 1948. Not even in kindergarten yet. But my mother was transformed. Young and modern, she was ready to reject the antiquated society where old men ruled from their coffee farms, and the poor—to quote her hero Don Pepe—hadn't conceived of another, better kind of life. A shallow undercurrent of politics soaked our house in the 1950s. Headlines became Mamá's five-second tutelage on ideas that were new to her. Women's suffrage! The rights of blacks! The rights of the poor! Politics was our prayer before every meal. The triumph of the middle class! Down with the oligarchy! Down with unbridled capitalism! Politics was our lullaby. Down with Yankee imperialism! Long live the Second Republic! *¡Viva siempre el trabajo y la paz!*

I hated politics, so did our father. Hernán, my little brother, born four years into the Second Republic, was still sucking his thumb when Papá—definitely not a modern man— gave up on hiding his extramarital affairs. Flitting from one woman to the next, until he started a new family with one of them and just didn't bother coming back to our house at night. We'd only see him when he'd come around to drop off remittances from Abuelito in Kentucky, with a few *colones* of his own thrown in to assuage his guilt. Mamá didn't suffer much; she, too, moved on to other partners, clinging to whichever political ideas those men would introduce to her.

In the room I shared with Hernán, I hid the postcards from Abuelito under my pillow. I made them only mine: the images of horses on green fields, the Welcome to Kentucky one with the cartoon Abraham Lincoln, the neat and orderly streetscape of Louisville. I would admire them before going to sleep. His postcards never talked of politics. They talked about work. And peace.

"Sponsor me, Abuelito," I asked him when I turned eighteen.

Abuelito had been sponsored by his sister Zoe's husband, Frank. Frank, a one-time US Army sergeant and proud-to-be an American, made sure Abuelito was for real, not some loafer who wanted to suckle at the teat of the great USA. He made sure Abuelito got his citizenship, paid his taxes.

"Okay, Juan Manuel," Abuelito said to me via long-distance phone. "But this is a country where you have to work hard to become great. Good old-fashioned hard work, and if you do that, the world is handed to you on a platter: a good wife, a nice house, a shiny car. Are you ready for that?"

Gone was the lover of Catholic socialism. Taking its place was a *nouveau* Puritan believer in the saving grace of hard work. He had succumbed to emigratory amnesia years earlier.

"Yes, Abuelito! I'm ready to start living," I said.

"Then, when you come here, let's call you, John," he concluded.

I didn't object.

Right before I left, I climbed a tree at a downtown San José avenue to get a better view over the heads of the tens of thousands of people who lined the streets to cheer on

President John F. Kennedy, the first US president to ever visit our little country. I could swear that my whistles of support were heard over the voices of others. I could swear that President Kennedy looked up at me. His name was my name, too.

∽∾∽

*1981*

"*Mi amorcito*, your brother needs you."

My mother's phone call came in just as I was leaving for work. I had chugged down some coffee, but it hadn't hit yet. My brain was blurry. I was in a rush.

"They arrested him this morning," she continued. She sounded like she had been crying.

That stopped me. "What? Who? Hernán?"

"Pay attention to me, Juan!" my mother scolded, her voice becoming urgent and angry. "Hernán was arrested. Things are going crazy here. They say he's been hanging out with communists. They killed his friend's girlfriend, Viviana, in her jail cell. You need to come home now. Hernán needs you."

Technically, I was home. Chicago, where Candace and I had moved after we got married in Louisville in 1971, she at twenty-two and me at twenty-seven. Candy was from a long line of Kentuckians for whom the four corners of the world had been limited to Dixie. Her blond hair and light eyes were as exotic to me as my perennially tanned skin was to her. We had both outgrown Louisville by the 1970s and Chicago, the big city, beckoned. We jumped into our car with the Just Married letters still smeared across the back window and set off for the six-hour ride north, looking for more space to spread our wings and find ourselves. We settled in a nice

115

apartment in Pilsen, disguising ourselves among the influx of Mexicans settling into the neighborhood of long-time Eastern European residents.

In Pilsen, I did find myself in the faces of other Central Americans who'd call me John but pronounce it *Yon*. "Speak English, y'all!" Candy would say sweetly at first, with a smile. Later, it became a little more forceful: "Speak English, John. I don't understand you." Finally, it became an angry murmur: "Goddammit. Speak English, y'all. This is America!"

We didn't last the whole of six years, despite our still-professed love.

"I just don't fit into your world," Candy said to me the day she hightailed it back to Louisville. She wore a Mexican blouse with flowers embroidered in riotous colors, a parting gift from our neighbor, Juanita.

I didn't stop her because I couldn't define my world with thick lines. I was an immigrant. I was an American. I was neither here nor there. I could be everywhere. And yet there I was, nearly four years later, home in the same small two-bedroom house that Candy and I had bought from an octogenarian Polish couple the year before we split. The neighborhood was increasingly Mexican. As a Costa Rican who had adopted an Anglo name and a navy-blue passport when bell-bottoms were in high style, I was comfortable enough straddling the shifting demographic ground. The Mexicans didn't exactly claim me. Neither did the white Americans. But I felt I belonged.

"Come as quickly as you can," my mother urged, before she hung up.

"John, don't get involved," Abuelito said, before I had finished relaying my conversation with Mom to him. Never having remarried, he was living out his twilight years with the widowed Zoe, still in Louisville. "I love Hernán, too. But

I've heard this story before: subversive types looking to upend the peace of the country."

He repeated one of his favorite cautionary tales to me, about how the Germans torpedoed a banana boat in Limón in 1942 and the communists organized a demonstration that Calderón spoke at. The crowd went wild, literally, and looted the shops owned by Germans, Italians and pro-Franco Spaniards. The government, it was said, did nothing.

"That was the doctor's one big mistake, letting the world's problems affect Costa Rica, and it opened the door to Figueres. But these ideas, now, these are more dangerous. These communist terrorists don't want a better Costa Rica. They want disorder, confusion. It's anti-American bullshit. I don't want you involved. You stay out. You're an American now. He'll bring you down."

I didn't listen. I'd love to say that it was solely brotherly altruism that drove me. In truth, that was only a small part of my decision to take a leave of absence to go to Costa Rica. The economy and Reagan's First 100-day search for "extravagance" in federal spending had put my job with the Chicago schools on notice. I crunched numbers for the school districts' lunch program, and if the folks in Washington decided kids were going to be eating less, there would be less money to count and some of us would have to go. Inflation, the impending cuts, politics were seeping into my everyday life again. I had already been wanting a change, anyway, but I hedged my bets and used Hernán as an excuse for a hastily planned vacation, plus an extra week's leave. I figured I'd hand in my resignation and look for a new job when I returned. At least, I wouldn't leave any vacation time on the table.

Talo and Juanita, my friends in the basement apartment next door, promised to look after my house while I was away and maybe even throw a party or two there. I left them my keys, anyway.

I arrived on July 15th, a week after Hernán's arrest, right in the middle of the rainy season, what we call winter in the isthmus. From the little round plane window, I could just make out the green of the peaks surrounding the valley in which we had landed, made gloomy by the low gray clouds and the rain splattering against the pane. It filled me with a heaviness that I masked with a big, fake smile when I emerged from the jetway.

Mamá, still pretty but looking older, smaller and grayer than I remembered, was there to greet me. Holding her hand and threatening to hide himself behind her was Randal, Hernán's eight-year-old son from his tragic marriage to what Mamá called "*la* hippie." Ingrid, his bride, was only nineteen when they had married. She wore her hair long and flowing, parted in the middle, halfway down her back, and favored long cotton dresses with ruffled hems. Hernán had been working as a uniformed civil guard when he met her. They were an odd pairing, but they fell madly in love. She was in college studying political science, but she dropped out when she found out she was pregnant, and they got married before the baby arrived. Randal was not even in school yet when she and Hernán crashed their car en route home from Sarapiquí. Hernán broke his leg in two parts. Ingrid, her forehead shattering the windshield, died instantly. Randal, who luckily was not in the car, inherited his mother's thick black hair, caramel skin and huge dark eyes.

He didn't remember me.

"Randalcito, little man!" I greeted him. My hand held up in a high five was left alone. He just stared at me, his big eyes blinking.

"Don't bother him," was my mother's greeting to me, with a hug. "He's shy."

I winked at him and mussed up his messy hair some and went with them to get my one suitcase.

Mamá glared at me when she saw it.

I put my arm around her shoulder and consoled her. "That's all I'm going to need, Mamá. It's going to be all right. We'll get this straightened out with Hernán in no time. He'll get out. He'll be fine, and then I'll go home," I said, soothingly. "I promise."

I'd rue those words.

∽∾∽

The three of us had spent that rainy first day hunkering down in Mamá's kitchen. Randal hadn't gone to school so he could go with his grandmother to get me at the airport. Without talking too much, he had pulled out his coloring books and colored pencils and invited me to color with him. We did that for a long spell while Mamá made us an elaborate feast of my favorite foods: *gallo pinto*, *maduros*, cabbage salad and thin steaks doused in Salsa Lizano. After our late lunch, we played some Chinese checkers, colored some more until it was suppertime, and Mamá let us do a TV dinner watching Kim Carnes' costumed *Bette Davis Eyes* video on *Hola Juventud*. She reminded me of Candy, and I got lost in thought. The last time I had been to Costa Rica was after my divorce, not long after Hernán had been widowed, and we buried our sorrow watching cartoons on the TV with Randal sitting on our laps.

"That's Papi's favorite song," volunteered Randal midway through the video. Without taking his eyes off the television, he added, "Papi is in jail."

He was wearing the new Captain America pajamas I had brought him, even though it wasn't quite bedtime. I took it as a compliment.

"I know, little man," was all I could manage to say.

His big eyes lingered on me, questioning, but I had no answers for him. We stared at the TV, watching Kim until her video morphed into Olivia Newton John doing aerobics in *Physical*.

Randal had been staying with Mamá since Hernán was hauled away, arrested in front of all his colleagues and employees at the Datsun dealership he managed. After he went to bed, she and I sat down at the table. I opened a beer, and she poured herself some chamomile tea.

"What happened, Mamá?"

"His friend, Érica, you know, the daughter of Jorge who owns Pulpería La Gloria . . ."

I shook my head, took a swig and waved my hand to signal her to carry on, not get lost in insignificant minutiae like she tended to do.

"It doesn't matter," she said impatiently, launching into the telling she had repressed from her friends and associates for shame or self-protection. "Érica called me that morning. Hernán had used his one call to call her. I don't know why. They're not even lovers. Or at least I don't think they are. But she called me and told me that there had been a misunderstanding, that Hernán had been arrested that morning as he arrived at work, and could I hold on to Randal after I picked him up from school."

"I didn't even know what to think. I kept asking her, why? What did he do? And she told me to calm down, that it was all a mistake. That the Department of Justice was out of their minds because Viviana had been assassinated. Viviana,

Carlos' girlfriend. Poor Carlos, who was also killed but out in the street.

"She said that now the Department of Justice investigators were seeing shadows everywhere. That the accusations against Hernán would come out in the wash.

"'What accusations?' I asked Érica. 'What did he do?' Érica kept telling me to relax, that he did nothing, that they were getting him help. I asked her over and over again who *they* were. She wouldn't answer. She just asked if I could pick up Randal and keep him until Hernán got home."

Mamá was quiet for a moment, then continued. "I don't understand. Poor Viviana, they said she was a terrorist. Who knows what she and Carlos were up to that night. He was killed in a shootout! Impossible to imagine. I'm not saying they deserved to die, but what did they have to do with Hernán? Nothing!"

I shook my head slowly, and my silence urged her on.

"You remember Carlos, right? He was that neighbor of your brother's when he and the hippie lived in Guadalupe. They were all in that university intellectual phase. I went to one of their parties back then, before Ingrid died. They were just kids! Politics, politics, politics all night long! They'd smoke and try to fix the world." She laughed at the memory. "But who am I to laugh? I loved that stuff when I was young. . . ."

"I vaguely remember him, Mamá. Nice guy. He made leather things, right?"

"Yes! That's him!" she said.

She got up and ran to get a folding three-legged stool with a worked leather seat that had broad white stitching and the words Costa Rica embroidered along one side. Patriotism embossed on leather; every family had something like that in their house. Or a vividly painted oxcart. Or decorative cutting boards made of multi-colored hardwoods. Or a coffee picker carved out of a stump of wood. All would be sure to have the words Costa Rica in a neat cursive. If I didn't know better, I'd have thought it was a civic obligation. But Ticos were reflexively proud, members of an exceptional experiment that worked, enjoying a reputation among foreigners as pacifists and educated. For those who delved deeper, the antithesis of Cuba.

"Carlos made this!" Mamá continued. "Hernán gave it to me a couple of Christmases ago. Beautiful! An artist, very nice boy. They were good friends. I'd see him every now and then. But a terrorist? I don't believe it. Maybe it was that girl, but I can't believe Carlos would have anything to do with terrorism.

"Érica said they arrested dozens of innocent people. They're looking for any excuse. They're trying to deflect the anger against Viviana's assassination. Here, I saved you all the papers."

I was exhausted. My beer was long finished. I excused myself, gave Mamá a kiss, promised to read a bit, keep talking in the morning and made to retire to Hernán's old bedroom.

"You're better off sleeping in my room. I'll sleep with Randal. I keep Hernán's room locked because it's a mess. It's become a closet. I just don't feel like dealing with it," she said. "I'll see you in the morning, *mi amor*. I'm glad you're here. We're his family. He needs our help."

I brought the stack of newspapers into bed with me. There were countless stories, analyses, sidebars and opinions. Viviana's assassination was the only thing that had happened in the country that month, it seemed. She had been mown down in her cell, right after she'd had her morning coffee, two weeks after her arrest. The twenty-three-year-old corporal, who had stuck the barrel of his automatic rifle in between the bars and sprayed her with bullets while her horrified cellmates dodged the ricochets, calmly handed his weapon over to a colleague and turned himself in. "What's done is done," he was reported to have said.

It was an unbelievable story. It was not the Costa Rica I knew. It was Nicaragua. El Salvador. Guatemala. But not us. And yet there it was in black and white. On June 12th, Viviana, Carlos and two other kids were parked in a yellow Datsun in Guadalupe. A patrol car pulled up to two men changing the license plate on that car, which had been reported stolen a few days earlier. Mayhem ensued. There was a shoot-out: three cops were shot dead. Carlos was shot in the forehead. With the injured Carlos in the passenger seat, the others in the back, Viviana drove the car away. A guardsman hopped into an idling taxi and ordered it to follow them. Along the way, the kids in the backseat vanished, and someone from the yellow Datsun (Viviana? The wounded Carlos? The fugitives?) shot and killed the taxi driver. Highways were shut down. Police sirens wailed all over. A dragnet was ordered for the yellow Datsun. The newspaper reports stated that when the car and driver were finally found, Viviana was trying to dump Carlos' body by the Torres River. Carlos was taken to the hospital, where he died. Viviana was locked up and held incommunicado.

Fourteen hours later, she had still not spoken. The police somehow surmised that her band of friends in the yellow Datsun were the tip of the spear, that they were part of a subversive group that had been committing acts of violence since March that year. These included the bombing of a van filled with US Marines and the bombing of the Honduran embassy. Also, some had attempted to blow up the statue of John F. Kennedy in San Pedro and had shot up a police car in

Zapote. According to the reports, Carlos and Viviana were linked to these, but they had not acted alone.

The press latched on, dehumanized them and labeled them communists and terrorists. They blamed the conservative President Rodrigo Carazo, stating it was his fault for having allowed radical anti-Somoza elements to thrive in Costa Rica during the Nicaraguan Revolution.

It was the presidential election season, and all the candidates were having a field day with this. The Liberación candidate called for building the political resolve to strike out terrorism. The right-wing candidate said he'd be the one who could put a stop to Marxists' penetration. Even the communists entered the fray, denouncing terrorism as a ploy of the ultrarightists. Calderón Guardia's son, who was a candidate that year, recommended more economic guarantees to improve the standard of living and avoid radicalization of young people.

That word struck me. *Radicalization.* What had Hernán gotten himself into?

Meanwhile, the country had been whipped up into a frenzy by the news reports and was seeing terrorists and fugitive yellow cars everywhere. People all over the city were reporting gunshots, and bands of police and Department of Justice teams were looking for terrorists under every rock. They said they raided a safe house in Goicoechea, hit pay dirt and used the reams of information they found there to carry out dozens more raids, in Zapote, Barrio Luján, Desamparados and other places all over the San José area. The insurgent group kept good notes, writing down details of their missions and even their failures. The notes described an organized group, with directors, soldiers and cells. In the end, more than thirty people were arrested from throughout the metropolitan area, and the Justice Department identified fifteen cells, each with four or five members. Their conclusion was that, since 1978, high school and university students had been recruited and groomed by what officials called "highly technified intellectuals." These were terrorists, Justice concluded, who called themselves La Familia.

Viviana, the terrorist, was killed. My brother, an accused terrorist, was in jail. I feared he would be next.

My head hurt. It was all too much. That night, I dreamt of yellow Datsuns with machine gun barrels coming out of its windows. I needed to talk with Hernán, but that would have to wait until Sunday, visiting day, if he wasn't released before then.

∽ ∽ ∽

The next day, Thursday, after we took Randal to school, Mamá and I walked the fifteen-minute route from her house in Arpaza to Hernán's house in Los Sauces. We passed by a large, recently sodded city block on Calle 60 that, when we were kids, had once marked the start of the gentle descent to the Río Tiribí through thicket and smallholder coffee plantings and people's yards with goats tethered, chickens pecking and an occasional stinky pigpen.

"Look at that new development," Mamá pointed out, not breaking her stride. "They chopped down everything green and then named it *Urbanización Florestal*. Imagine that! They bought all the land down there. It's going to be big. But for now, there are all these empty lots and new houses waiting for people to buy them. Bad timing, but people have been moving in. Even *gringos!*"

"The trees will grow back, Mamá. It'll be a nice park," I said, not terribly affected one way or another by the country's recent economic downturn. "It's progress. We can't keep pretending we're an old-fashioned country of coffee farmers."

Hernán's neighborhood also bore the scars of stalled new development, but his house was on a block built in the early 1970s, and there were sidewalks and some trees, and ladies doing their morning sweeping of driveways. There were choruses of *"¡Buenos días!"* as we walked past. Mamá unlocked a chain holding closed the gate to Hernán's driveway. At his door, I noticed that the lock was hanging on for dear life, and the wood was splintered and cracked.

"The Justice officers busted in after they arrested him. They said they were looking for evidence," Mamá said in disgust. "The neighbors are so worried for him. They really look out for him and Randal . . . bringing them food, as if they were poor. They just feel bad that they're alone, like bachelors."

Inside was a disaster. Couch cushions had been slashed, their stuffing littering the room. The wooden room divider had been knocked onto the dining room table, with pieces of plates and knick-knacks everywhere, crunching underfoot. Every kitchen cabinet and drawer had been opened, and their contents strewn unceremoniously. The same in the bathroom. Hernán's bedroom and office were impassable: clothes, bedding, mattress stuffing, papers, boxes and pictures everywhere, even spilling out into the tiny hallway. Ceiling tiles were randomly punched in along the way.

Strangely, the door to Randal's little bedroom, across the hall from Hernán's, was shut. When I opened it, I was struck by the relative neatness within. The bedspread and sheets were mangled on top of the child's foam mattress, and some toys that lived under the bed had been pulled out. The small closet doors were opened, and the clothes shoved aside. But aside from that, the tiny oasis of childhood had been spared. Above, the elaborate mobiles of the solar system and constellations of stars dangled from seemingly every inch of the ceiling and rotated gently. Seeing them soothed me and, despite the disaster surrounding us, made me smile.

While I admired the display my brother had created for his son, Mamá had gone to grab cleaning supplies: brooms and pans and garbage bags.

"At least they mostly spared poor Randal," she said. "But let's get to work. Tomorrow is Friday. They usually free people before the weekend. Your brother has been through enough. Let's get this cleaned up so that he doesn't have to see it like this.

"You know, they came to my house last week, too" she added casually, while we picked up broken bits of Hernán's house. "But I did not let them search. No, sir: I was not going to let them do that to me. I've done nothing. Now, if they want to get on me about things I did in '48, well, it's too late. But I've done nothing now."

She kept sweeping and rambling on.

"You know who had the nerve to show up that day? Edgar! Remember Edgar Castillo? He was that man I was with a few years back. You remember him. So handsome . . . tall, thick black hair and a good mustache, *moreno* . . . the one who worked with the Justice Department? Oh! He's the one who recommended your brother to the civil guard, remember him?"

"Yeah, Mamá, yeah, I do." I remembered him as a macho guy, bit of a bully. She was dating him when Candy and I got married.

"Well, Edgar was wonderful. Such a gentleman. His wife, well, that's a different story. But in the end, he listened to her blah, blah, blah, and I couldn't stand it anymore. She was insufferable! So, I sent him packing.

"Well, he turns up with this Justice team of hacks the day after they arrested Hernán. At least they had the decency to knock and not just bust open the door, like they did here. And there's Edgar. And he's gorgeous as usual and he says, 'I'm sorry, Doña Judith'—he calls me Doña Judith! I guess he had to make it look professional, but Doña Judith!—So he says, 'I'm sorry, Doña Judith, but we are obligated to search your house.' 'For what?' I ask him. 'For evidence linking Hernán to the terrorists,' he says, staring at his feet. I lost it. 'Edgar! How could you think that?!!' I scolded him. He apologized, mumbled something to his guys, and they came in and stood in the living room, closing the door behind them. He nodded at them, and they went through the house, carefully opening the doors of the rooms and peeking in, opening the drawers and peeking in them. They made me unlock Hernán's room, but I hadn't changed the burnt-out lightbulb in there, so they couldn't turn the light on. They didn't bother to open the curtains, but Edgar asked me what all the boxes were. 'Just some of the stuff from when my sons were kids,' I said, and that was that. I didn't even offer him coffee. I was so mad at him. 'I'm sorry, Judith,' he said as he was leaving and stopped to kiss my cheek once his men were outside."

"Unbelievable, Mamá," I said, and I meant it.

We kept on working in silence. I was lost in thought, wondering about the madness that seemed to have befallen the country: terrorists everywhere, in yellow cars and children's closets and old lovers' living rooms.

We did the best we could with the time we had. We swept up the mess, gathered up the contents of drawers and put them away, in no particular order. We righted the furniture, and Mamá collected the stuffing and made Frankenstein stitches in the cushions to hold it in. We flipped those onto their intact sides for appearance's sake. We dragged his ruined mattress out back into the laundry room.

"We can go get him a new one tomorrow morning," she said, "and you can borrow a car to drive this one to the trash."

I said I'd return later in the day with a ladder to do what I could to put the ceiling tiles back in order and finish making the house look almost normal. But we were on borrowed time. We had to pick Randal up from school, and I had planned to meet Érica and get more information.

I had a quick lunch, and Mamá gave me directions to Érica's house. Hers was one of the new builds in Florestal, on the eastern side of the fledgling park, across from the pay phone and the taxi stand and along a freshly built boulevard with saplings in the median. Her driveway and garage had been converted into a *pulpería*, and I entered through there. She was waiting for me.

"Pleasure to meet you, Érica," I said and kissed her cheek in greeting.

"Oh, I know you already! Hernán has told me all about you. We're not strangers," she replied.

There were no customers at that hour, and her father was taking his lunch break. She and I pulled over two chairs and sat down in the middle of the shop. I told her I was short on time because I wanted to get back to Hernán's to find a way to fix the ceiling tiles in case he was released the next day. She fetched a cold Coca-Cola, opened it and handed it to me.

"Don't hurry," she said, flatly. "I'm glad you're here. I didn't know how to tell Doña Judith. Juan, they've thrown the book at Hernán. Twelve charges, including terrorism, treason, illegal association, attempted murder. . . . He's not getting out tomorrow. He's going to have to stand trial. They all are. They might even be charged with murder! The latest rumors in the press are that this 'subversive' gang is the one that ordered Viviana killed to keep her from talking . . . some Cold War conspiracy theories like that. Total idiocy."

"Érica, what were you guys involved in? What did Hernán do?"

"Nothing, Juan. He did nothing but dream for a better future for Costa Rica, for our brothers and sisters in Central America. He is a prisoner of conscience. He is not a terrorist." She was emphatic and sought to persuade me with her details.

She'd met both Hernán and Carlos in the past few years when she was in her last year of high school. Hernán and Carlos, who had been friends since the early 70s, were intoxicating for her young mind just waking up to the consciousness of wanting a better world, a more equitable Costa Rica, she said. Carlos had been a neighbor of Ingrid's since childhood, and Hernán had easily been folded into his friend group. They were a brainy bunch. Most, like Ingrid, had been university students, and they'd sit around each other's houses discussing big ideas. They dreamt of utopias, of a better, more equal world, where the campesino and the poor would have the same rights and standard of living as the university student, she said. Carlos had even gone to Cuba to see firsthand the promise and success of socialism there.

"Then the wars started," she said. "First Nicaragua. Then El Salvador."

The friends made more like-minded friends, and those friends made their own friends. Then, they all made plans, separate but united. First, like most Ticos, they rallied behind the Sandinistas.

"Down with the autocrats!" Érica said.

She hadn't met a soul who didn't want to see Somoza lose to the Sandinistas. They'd go out to San Carlos and Guanacaste and help those fighters who were training or stopping for air in Costa Rica, giving them food and camaraderie. Only after they won were some of their fellow Ticos turned off by the Sandinistas, but not *their* group, she said, not the idealists.

The freedom fighters were the future of the isthmus, and they believed that the anti-autocratic Farabundo Martí Liberation Front could achieve a similar victory in El Salvador. They believed that it was their duty to make sure this happened.

"That's what Carlos and Viviana were doing that night, Juan. They were transporting the guns to the Salvadoran buyers," she said.

The guns, leftovers from the war in Nicaragua, seeped over the border. These friends, the ones the press had dubbed La Familia, were doing the right thing and selling them to the Salvadoran opposition fighters.

"But Hernán and I weren't involved in any operations. We just organized meetings, you know. Places where we could all exchange ideas. I didn't know Viviana. We liked to keep things separate, you know. It was safer that way. But Carlos would tell us about her, like she was a superstar. 'Viviana said this,' or 'Viviana said that.' She was just nineteen. But she was intense. Too intense. After we had met her, I told Hernán that. I said she was not good for Carlos."

"Érica, you're talking about groups and guns and training fighters," I said. "You're talking about communists! That's not good. What were you thinking? You want Costa Rica to become Cuba or the Soviet Union? Were you all going crazy?"

I was shocked. The casual way that Érica bandied about the words "socialism" and "communism" and the "people united" never being defeated was just too much for me.

Érica just stared at me, looking hurt. She got up, walked around the store, straightened out a couple of packages and sat down again, like she couldn't remember what she had gotten up for in the first place. Then she put her hand on my hand.

"Costa Rica is unique, Juan. Our system is unique. You should know that. We're a democracy. We have a mixed economy. We have socialism. That's what has set us apart. And, yes, even the acceptance of communist ideas," she said, emotionally. "It's not about labels, Juan. It's about justice. What is right and fair."

"Well, it sure sounds like communism to me," I said.

"So what? If it sounds like the right thing to do, then who cares what label is put on it? 'Socialism,' 'communism' . . . they're not bad words, you know. Even Jesus would approve. The labels serve the bankers, the elite, the *yanquis* . . . the labels are their bugaboos," she said. "Hernán always said you wouldn't understand. He said that you had fallen too much in love with the Americans. That you had been blinded by them."

"Bullshit, Érica. There's right and there's wrong, and bringing war to Costa Rica is wrong," I said emphatically, hurt by my brother's accusation. "But enough. I need to know how to get Hernán out of there. You say he was not involved in more than talk. Okay. Let's tell the judge. Someone must know someone who's listening. Let's bring him home."

"It's not going to be that easy," she said. "He's going to have to stand trial. He's got a good lawyer. We made sure of that. This guy is representing a bunch of them. It just might take a few more weeks. I need you to explain that to your mother. And whatever you need, whatever she needs, please, call me."

Mamá did not take it too well. She cried and cried. Hernán had had enough heartbreak in his life, she said. This was too much for him, and too much for Randal. If only she had known with whom he was involved! She carried on about how she, too, had gotten caught up in the revolutionary fervor in the late 1940s, how that had energized her, how exciting it had been to be actively involved in the fight.

"It was fun," she said. "I thought Hernán was also filled with the spirit of '48. I thought it was giving him moral purpose. Don Pepe always said you could be a leftist without being a communist. He's right, of course. That's what Hernán was. I never thought he'd be accused of being a radical, a communist. *¡Jamás!* I would not have let that happen."

I promised to visit Hernán on Sunday so we could get a better picture, straight from the horse's mouth.

I didn't bother returning to his house that night. Instead, Randal and I watched TV for a while, sitting close together on the sofa before he went to bed.

∾ ∾ ∾

That Sunday, I left early. Hernán had been transferred earlier that week from the holding cells, where Mamá had visited him after his intake, to the federal prison in Alajuela. That should have been the cue to us that he would not be getting out any time soon.

Once there, I submitted to a strip search before being let into a large communal room set up with tables and chairs. There, wives and girlfriends wept across the table from their jailed men, and some of us men bore our worry stoically, arms crossed, brows furrowed. It was not a quiet room; a cacophony of conversations and crying and even laughter permeated.

Hernán was at a table already waiting for me. We embraced before a guard reminded us gruffly to sit across from each other without touching.

"*¿Pura vida?* I had to get you to come visit somehow, didn't I," he joked.

"You could have thought of a way better idea than becoming a revolutionary outlaw," I joked back.

"Put your bullhorn down," Hernán said, looking around surreptitiously. He lowered his voice to a little above a whisper. "We're not too popular here right now. The media has made us out to be monsters. The people are ignorant. They believe whatever they're told."

"So, tell me then, is it true? Are you a communist?" I asked in a voice above a whisper. I looked around. No one was paying us any mind, not even the guard who was chatting up another guard, both of their bodies blocking the doorway.

He laughed out loud. "Don't bust my balls, Juan! Please. What a dumb question. As if that were still a crime! You know what my 'crime' is? Dreaming of a better world. Like John Lennon, 'Imagine all the people, sharing all the world . . .'" he sang that line in terrible English.

"I don't want to get you in trouble," I said, lowering my voice a little more. "But explain all this to me. I talked to Érica. She went on and on about groups and meetings and actions, but she swears up and down that it was peaceful. That it was about going out and empowering campesinos, feeding the hungry. That at worst it was receiving the guns from the Nicas and handling the sale to the Salvadorans. All love and peace and shit. . . . But nothing about guns and Sandinistas and fighting in El Salvador sounds peaceful to me. And then she said that the right hand didn't know what the left hand was doing. That there were a lot of little groups, all loosely organized but only tied to each other, with someone—she doesn't know who—in charge of the whole thing and serving as the communicator with all the groups. I don't know, Hernán, but that sounds exactly like what the press has described."

"You're kidding me, man. Who are you going to believe, the right-wing press or your own brother? The Department of Justice? They're the same people who were out there helping our brothers fighting to liberate Nicaragua, giving them space on ranches in Guanacaste to train, covering up their presence when the OAS came sniffing around. Isn't this still the president who let the Group of Twelve use San José as their base, to spread the word that it wasn't the Sandinistas who were terrorists, that Somoza was the terrorist. Everyone, Juan, everyone in Costa Rica supported the Sandinistas. The southern front was, like the *gringos* say, a melting pot: there were Social Democrats, there were Marxists, there were conservative groups opposing Somoza. And we Ticos were cheering them on. And now? We have our brothers and sisters in El Salvador fighting the same fight, fighting for freedom, and what? Now we're terrorists for wanting to help them?

"Even Don Pepe supported them. The Somozas were his archenemies forever. And we all believed him when he said that Costa Rica was nothing like its neighbors and would never need a revolution because we had education and the media, and the two would ensure peace. We believed that we could make change, we could ward off war at our door, just by using our words. But the people weren't listening. And now the media is out there using words against us, saying that we're terrorists, telling the whole country that they need to band together to make sure the big, bad communists don't make inroads in our peaceful country. . . ."

I wanted to stick my fingers in my ears, like when I was a boy and Mamá or her latest boyfriend was schooling us in politics, but Hernán just kept going on and on.

"Did you know that of all my friends, only Érica has come to visit me?" he whispered, no longer ranting. "Only Érica. Everyone else is afraid. They're afraid to be labeled terrorists. They're afraid they'll get arrested, too. Even Érica is afraid, and she's just a secretary at the university's student affairs office. What's our country coming to when a secretary becomes afraid to speak her political mind?"

"It's just . . . it's just, when did you become so radicalized? You've got this perfect country, peace and love and family, education and good health. What more do you want? Why are you trying to ruin it?"

"Man, you sound just like a *gringo*. This is not Utopia! Did you know your boyfriend, Uncle Sam, has already invaded Nicaragua? Of course, you don't know. You *gringos* are so nice and warm, living in a house high on a hill away from it all. But when you feel pressure in the north, it pushes south and becomes a violent wind swooping into our valley, wreaking havoc. Our lives get blown about. We suffer, man. The people are sleeping."

"But guns and war are never the answer, brother."

He was quiet for a moment, then said, "I don't want to see war in Costa Rica. I want to see the people wake up and pay attention. They called us terrorists," and he winced as he said this. "I'm no terrorist, Juan. I think. That's my crime. I think."

"I'm sorry, Hernán. You know politics is not my thing. I've never even bothered to vote. This all has been a lot to take in within just a few days. Érica says your lawyers are on it. That once you have a hearing, you'll get a trial date and there you can prove your innocence, and we can put this behind us," I said, grabbing his hand. "Are you okay? Is there anything you need."

"It's boring here, but nothing I can't handle. They allow us books, and we play chess to pass the time," he said. "But I need you to do me a big favor for the next couple of weeks, until this is all over. Can you please take Randal back to our house and take care of him for me? I'm sure Mamá has been great, but I don't want this to affect his life too much. I want things to be as normal as possible for him."

"Of course, I can. You got it. I'll stick around for a couple more weeks, and Randal and I will have a great time together. In fact, I'm looking forward to getting to know him. He's shy, but we're becoming friends already."

"I can't thank you enough. But Juan, don't make him into a *gringo*, okay?"

We spent the rest of the visit talking about everything else but the elephant in the room. We figured the lawyers would take care of it all, and, I think, we were both exhausted by the topic.

When I got back to San José, I told Mamá of Hernán's request.

"Fix the house, then you can take him," she said. "He shouldn't see it like that."

∾ ∾ ∾

It took me three days to fix the house up. I had workers replace the ceiling tiles and install a new front door. I bought a new mattress and dumped the ruined one. By the middle of the week, Mamá and I walked Randal over after lunch—he always had lunch at her house, anyway, since Hernán didn't always make it home for lunch. He went straight to his room and checked on his toys. We left him alone for a bit, and when I went to check on him, he was lying face up on his bed, tears streaming from his eyes, staring into space.

"When is he coming home, Tío," was all he asked me.

"I don't know, little man. But how about this, let's go visit him together on Sunday, huh? Would you like that?"

I didn't need to wait for his answer. Later, I called Érica and asked her if she would lend me her car on Sunday so that

I wouldn't have to rent another one when I took Randal to see his father.

"I've got a better idea," she said. "Let me go with you."

And that's what we did. All of us, including Mamá. We packed up the car like we were going to the beach. Mamá prepared all of Hernán's favorite dishes and packed them in containers. Randal made a bunch of drawings and stapled them together, creating a comic book for his father. Once there, we were told at the door that the prisoner could not accept any food.

"I cooked this myself for my son," Mamá insisted. "Are you calling me a criminal? Why on earth would you not let me feed my son?"

I tried to calm her, but she was Mamá. When the guard told her that she could leave the containers right there and retrieve them on her way out, she accused him of wanting to eat her food because he was a shameless thief, and she'd be damned if she let him scarf down food made with love for her son. Then, she dramatically lifted the tops off the Pyrex bowls and dumped the food into an open trash can. Next, she put the dripping containers on the table and hissed, "I'll be back for these later. My son is innocent; you're the ones who are bad."

Ignoring her behavior as if they'd seen it a million times before, they let Randal bring in his comic book.

Hernán was incredibly happy to see his son. The first thing they did together was read the book he had made. Despite our hunger—we had stupidly not eaten enough in anticipation of the feast we had planned with Hernán—we had a wonderful time. We talked about anything and every-thing, from music to movies to the weather. If it weren't for the other prisoners or the guards, it would have felt like a typical Sunday afternoon at home, after lunch, when people gather and reconnect before the workweek ahead.

We left, saying we'd see him at home within the week.

I had been in Costa Rica for two weeks already. I had planned to be heading home in a week, two tops, but there had still been no movement on Hernán's hearing by the middle of that next week.

"Érica, what are they waiting for?" I asked her at the *pulpería*.

"They say they've gotten all the 'documentation' of the group, that they've had it since mid-June. I don't know what 'documentation' they're talking about because there is no documentation that I ever saw, and I'm a secretary! There is no 'organized terrorist group.' But whatever. It doesn't matter what I think. They say they have everything, but there's too much media attention, and the judges say that's preventing them from setting a trial date," she said. "Can you believe that? The judges are saying that all this media craze means they can't ensure a fair trial. Bullshit! They're using them to set an example, to warn people to toe the party line, to not think for themselves. They're using them to show off to the fucking *yanquis*. Give us money and we'll give you communists.' Fucking *yanquis*!"

Then she looked at me apologetically. "Sorry, Juan," she said. "But you don't count. You're a Tico, not a *yanqui*."

We had no idea when Hernán would get out. And my vacation was coming to an end.

"Well, in that I am not rich, I'm definitely Tico, not *gringo*," I said. "I promised Hernán I'd stay to be with Randal until he got out, but I can't be on vacation forever. I cannot afford not to work. And there's my house. I have to pay for it, I can't abandon it."

There was nothing either of us could say. She just shrugged.

"Look, if I can find you a job here, do you think you can stay a while longer?" she asked.

That was not part of the plan. I wanted to go home. But I couldn't do that to Randal, or Hernán.

"Well, put out some feelers, just in case," I told her.

Hernán was not upbeat at all that Sunday.

"They're not letting me read the papers in here, brother," he said by way of greeting.

"Don't worry. You're not missing out on anything. Same ol' same ol'. War and money, that's all it ever is. Nothing changes. It's been like that forever."

"See, that's where you're wrong. Things can change if we want them to, if we work for it. We have to unite as a people . . ."

"Oh brother! Here we go again!" I cut him off. "I have no interest in communist indoctrination today."

"Open your mind, Juan. Dream a little."

"Dreams don't need to include revolutionary intrigue, brother."

"This country, the Second Republic, was founded on revolutionary intrigue!" he said.

He and Erica talked of the Second Republic in a way that was new to me. Some of the old folks, like Abuelito, would reminisce about those times, but for most of us, it was just ancient history. Hernán would launch into recaps of the revolution like it was Sunday's soccer report. He'd punctuate conversations with commentary on how the elites hated Calderón Guardia because he dared to enshrine the needs of the common man. How despite their support, Figueres hated the elites because they were keeping the country hostage in some old-fashioned bygone world, so he screwed them over and nationalized banks and industries, built up the middle class and still hung on to Calderón Guardia's social safety net.

"Don't you remember that from history class?"

"Oh my God. You sound like Mamá!" I laughed out loud. "That all sounds like good stuff to me. So why can't you people just leave it alone already?"

He scoffed at me.

He'd hold forth like a professor, this car-dealer brother of mine. His recall of history class lessons, of recent history or family lore or news stories was impressive. I wondered out loud if he had become a proselytizer among the jail inmates. He just laughed away my question with a chuckle and a wave of his hand. But he didn't skip a beat and finished what he was trying to explain.

"Did you know that in 1948, Mamá once hid guns under her bed to slip them to the Figueristas? A favor for a neighbor. Papá didn't even know. She wasn't the only one. Everyone picked a side and got involved. You weren't here in 1978, but the Sandinista revolution was like that, too. Everyone was fired up, and we all agreed: Somoza and his murderous regime had to go. The autocrats were keeping the people down. That's when I really got involved, beyond discussion groups on Sundays with Ingrid and friends or listening to Carlos go on and on about his trip to Cuba and what he learned there. . . ."

He and Ingrid had promised each other to always work toward a fairer world for Randal, even before he was born. "This was always part of our plan," he said. ". . . A world we could be proud of."

"So communist dictators in Nicaragua are your idea of a fair world?" I taunted, then lowered my voice to a near whisper and added, "A fairer world is your friend and his girlfriend shooting cops to get guns to El Salvador so a war can be waged there?"

We both looked around furtively, to make sure no one was listening to us.

"We don't know what happened. They were both killed, and all we have is the police's story," he said in a hushed tone. "Remember, I was with the Civil Guard for a while before the accident. I know what they're like. I think they targeted Carlos and Viviana because they were pissed that someone had shot at them in Zapote, and they wanted to get revenge. The Civil Guard is not made up of thinkers. They're just cops with bigger guns. And you know, the National Assembly said so themselves: they're corrupt."

In an investigation earlier that year, the president hadn't denied that Costa Rica had allowed some arms traffic, out of a sense of national commitment, during the Nicaraguan war. That same investigation didn't do much to dispel the rumors, Hernán said, that the Civil Guard had stolen a bunch of the 5,000 Belgian FALs that were sent by Venezuela and Panama for the Sandinistas. In exchange for safe passage, the Civil Guard and some others skimmed twenty-five percent of those guns off the top, to sell later for a profit.

"There's a war raging next door, and their brothers need those weapons to survive, and they steal them to sell them to make a few bucks. You've gotta be kidding!" he said. "But the joke is on everyone because those guns weren't from Panama and Venezuela, they were from Cuba. Carlos told me that."

"Shhhh, let's change the subject," I said.

I looked around, but as usual, no one was paying attention to us. We were invisible among the prisoners and visitors, everyone isolated in their own tragedies.

"Remember when we were little and Mamá would sit on the edge of our beds at night and make us say our prayer to *Niñito Jesus*? Then, instead of saying amen at the end, she'd make us sing the last line of the national anthem: '*Viva siempre el trabajo y la paz.*' And she'd wave her hands like a conductor?" We both chuckled at that memory. "The line she should have made us repeat every night was the one that we repeat twice in that anthem: 'Eternal prestige, respect and honor.'"

"Man! Costa Rica is fine! Don't be so dramatic!" I raised my arms in exasperation, leaned back in my chair and guffawed. "Everyone can read. You get sick, you go to the doctor. You get old, you get a pension. Look at you. You have a nice house, a nice car, a good job, you take vacations to the beach. Everyone I know in Costa Rica lives the good life. Sometimes I get a little jealous. It has crossed my mind that if I had stayed, I wouldn't have to worry about wars in Asia, or oil embargos, or nuclear holocausts, or, dammit, budget cuts that mean I won't have a job soon. I get a whole two weeks off out of the year—two weeks, that's it! I don't understand you, man. Who's disrespecting you? Most people in the United States can't even place this country on a map, so I can guarantee you they're not the ones trying to steal your prestige, respect or honor. They don't even know you exist."

"See, that's where you drive me crazy. You leave because you say you hate politics. You embrace the slogans as if they explain everything. Your America is *pura vida*, live and let live, right? But here in Latin America, your America is our abusive lover who insists that without them we'll be nothing. We'll never be loved like they love us. And we start to believe them. But behind our back, they say the same thing to their other lovers, and they're ready to dump all of us if we don't give them the only thing they really want: all our money, more power and our souls. You can't hate what you don't know anything about, Juan."

"I learned plenty in history. And here's what sticks: 1. Democracy, not dictators and 2. Communism is the enemy.

143

You know what? That's all I still care about. The rest . . . the intrigue, the politics, the fights . . . just give me freedom and get out of my way. Don't tread on me."

Debates like these angered me. Why would he choose to complicate what should have been a nice, easy life? But my arguments always fell flat. He never gave me even an inch.

"Wow, you really did give in. You let your boyfriend Uncle Sam give it to you! And I bet he does a good job!" he said, laughing. "Tell me: How do you like taking it up the ass?"

"Up yours, brother!" I said, laughing.

At least I got him to smile a little and laugh, but it bothered me deeply that he couldn't just leave well enough alone. Ever. He couldn't accept imperfection. Nothing was just good enough.

He quickly got serious again. "I have a bad feeling about this, Juan. They're turning us into symbols, boogeymen. We're all going to end up like Carlos and Viviana."

"Nah, don't go down that road. Don't let them get you down. If you do, they win. Stay positive. This will end. I'm not leaving until it does. I promise."

My own words stranded me in Costa Rica.

∽∽∽

When I called my neighbors in Pilsen, Talo and Juanita, to tell them that I was stuck, they were understanding. Comings and goings were part of the immigrant experience, and some-times, like me, people got stuck.

"Listen, our lease is up at the end of the month. Mind if we live in your place until you come back?" asked Talo.

"'*Mano*, I can't let you have it for free. Pay the mortgage for me, and we'll call it even. It will be cheaper than renting it. And take good care of it."

I put a resignation letter in the mail for my job. I wasn't too sad about that. I was probably going to get laid off anyway, so I didn't give it too much thought.

Érica came through for me. Through her university post, she got me a job selling and delivering books for the national university book publisher. She also made the rounds to get Hernán's blue Datsun station wagon released from the impound. It was clean as a whistle, they said.

Only when I knew everything was going to work out did I tell Randal. His reaction was a big smile. We had settled into a bachelor routine in the evenings. He'd do his homework after I picked him up from Mamá's, and then we'd sit down to watch a little television, some *Mazinger Z* for the cartoon thrills and *Hola Juventud* for escapism. We both loved that show! I'd sing along to the songs I knew in English, and together we'd sing the Spanish ones. Every now and then, he'd stop to tell me his father liked this or that song. And he'd never let me sing along to Kim Carnes.

"Quiet," he'd say. "That's Papi's song."

"I get it," I'd reply. And I'd think about Candy.

One night after our bachelor routine at the beginning of September, I lay in his twin bed with him staring into space, as we usually did. He was a little sad that night.

"Before he turned off the lights, Papi always said that if we reach high enough, we'll always find a better world past the stars," he said. "I don't think Papi is going to be here for my birthday."

Randal's birthday was on Independence Day, September 15. In the past, he always had a day off from school for the country-wide celebration.

145

I had decided not to give the boy false hope. "No," I said. "I don't think so either."

"He doesn't know this, but before he went to jail, I heard him and Érica hiding my birthday present. They were whispering in my room, and when I opened one eye, I saw him standing on a ladder. She was giving him a box. He put it up there, above the Big Dipper. I knew it was my birthday present, and I didn't want him to think I was cheating, so I closed my eyes tight and didn't let them know I was awake. But Tío Juan, I really, really want my birthday present. It was a big box. I wish Papi could come home to give it to me. Could you ask him on Sunday? Tell him not to be mad at me for cheating and ask him if you can give it to me, instead."

I stared up at the Big Dipper. "Sure, Randal. I'll ask him."

I almost forgot to.

Hernán and I had been reminiscing and laughing throughout that visit. We were making fun of all of Mamá's boyfriends over the years and how she had a predilection for married men. I told him about Edgar searching Mamá's house, all awkward about it, and how they barely even opened the drawers because he was so embarrassed to be there. He raised his eyebrows and shook his head.

We laughed about the awkwardness of Papá's visits to drop off money, especially when one of the boyfriends was sitting at the dinner table. He filled me in on Papá, with whom he had grown somewhat close, it seemed, in his adulthood. I was a little jealous, but then I was closer to Abuelito than he was.

Talking about Abuelito led us to talk about his ardent Calderonismo. I told him how excited Abuelito was about Reagan's election. "The cowboy," he'd say, beaming, and I'd laugh and have to remind him that he just played a cowboy in the movies.

"I don't know how you got yourself mixed up in this shit. I still really, really hate politics," I said to Hernán. "I mean, what a waste of time! Mamá's sloganeering did a job on me. You couldn't say anything without her grabbing the newspaper and poking at some headline or other. She never would read the stories, just the headlines. She never cared what the story said. So long as it sided with Don Pepe, she was good. I've been thinking about what you said the other day and wondering why Mamá actually cared so much about Figueres that she'd risk hiding guns under her bed."

"Ah, Mamá is complicated. I think she just wanted to be free of Papá and Abuelito and all the traditions, and be modern," he said. "You know, she was exactly the same during the Nicaraguan Revolution. She picked her side, the Sandinistas like everyone else, and then she turned on them the minute all the conversative newspapers started publishing headlines that the Sandinistas were bad.

"Mamá loved Figueres because he seemed modern. And don't get me wrong, he did a lot of things right. But he cozied up to the Americans, bragging that through his friendship with the capitalists and the *yanquis,* he could convince them. 'Utopian socialism,' that's what it's called, fighting the battle from within through persuasion, and he said he was going to make Figuerismo our own unique version. Perfectly adapted for us, for this country. But this idea, it's a fantasy, like the blue morpho butterfly that's not blue at all. When it needs to blend in, to camouflage, it's brown. When it wants to send a signal, it just looks blue. Its scales play a trick of light on our eyes. Iridescence: it becomes what it wants you to see, when it wants you to see it, depending on your angle.

"So sure," he explained, "the state bought up the means of production, gave people jobs and doctors and education. But any time anyone complained that maybe the bourgeoisie was getting a better deal than the campesino, what did the state do? Nothing. It would just create another agency to study the problem and borrow money to keep that afloat.

"He pretended we'd be different, but it was an illusion," Hernán continued with his litany. "And all that money we borrowed? The *yanquis* gave it as gifts with long strings attached, just as expected. They were never going to give up power and they were persuaded of nothing. Now, they think they own us and can tell us how to live."

"So, what's the alternative, Hernán? You want Moscow to tell you how to live? You want to solve everything with violence? "

"You're missing the point, Juan," he said, pointing out that ever since Kennedy came and said that all Central America was going to work together to make sure Cuba failed, the only metric had been money and riches, not the well-being of the people. In fact, he noted, Nicaragua and El Salvador had more economic growth than Costa Rica in the 1960s and 70s, but no one really knew that because the money had been distributed so unevenly.

"Look at them now! The rich are richer than your wildest dreams, and 99 percent of the people there are miserable," he said. "But we're headed in the same direction. We Ticos are now fucked. We dug a hole for ourselves playing with fire, taking capital from your Uncle Sam, because he only takes as payment obedience or ownership. The *yanquis* have never been out to build utopias. They only want what makes them richer and allows them to pull the strings on their puppets most effectively."

We sounded like, I imagined, what his friends sounded like in their discussion groups, like the one Mamá had witnessed when Ingrid was still alive: salons fueled by beer and cigarettes, debating ideas, history, solutions to non-problems, solutions to real problems. We'd talk for hours during those jailhouse visits. He'd get up on his soapbox and stay there forever. I wasn't bored. My mind would drift, but his words would penetrate like those of a good teacher forced to lecture on subjects his students didn't want to learn. Hernán's jabbering would make me think about his ideas long after I'd left the visiting hall and had driven home from Alajuela. The thoughts he provoked followed me into my daily routines.

"Okay, to avoid the risk of becoming superficial, like Mamá, I will let you, little brother, explain something to me," I said during that Sunday's discussion, comically condescendingly. "How on earth can you support a government that pretends to want people to get power—such as Nicaragua—but then just becomes another dictatorship and lets people suffer and go hungry?"

He laughed. "That can't be a real question! You actually believe your adopted capitalist country cares about you, let alone us poor Ticos? No way. They own you, man. If you're so worried about dictatorships of the proletariat, consider what you live under. It's not a democracy, it's a dictatorship of the bourgeoisie."

I audibly groaned and rolled my eyes. These political conversations energized Hernán. When I'd leave him, I would notice his spirits higher than when I first arrived, the intellectual workout bringing a flush to his face. It was the least I could do.

I had stood to leave when I remembered Randal's request.

"Oh, Hernán, I almost forgot!" I told him what Randal said to me, laughing at his fear that Hernán would be mad at him. "So, if you don't mind, I'll get the gift down and wrap it up for him."

Hernán's face froze for a split second. "That little devil . . . The things he dreams up! He's going to be a writer someday," he said. "There's no present in the ceiling for him. He must have been dreaming. But hey, can you go buy him a soccer ball and give it to him for me? He'll love that!"

"Sure," I said. But something about that momentary hesitation on his part triggered a wave of doubt in me.

∽∾∽

After I dropped Randal off at school the next day, instead of heading to work, I returned to Hernán's house. I grabbed the ladder from the laundry room out back and took it to Randal's bedroom. I closed the door and locked it. I don't know why I did that, but I did. I climbed up to the Big Dipper and pushed lightly against the tile there. It gave easily. There was nothing over it. I pushed it over and was immensely relieved that I was able to easily slide it over.

What was wrong with me? Why was I doubting him? I stood there at the top of the ladder, head hanging, feeling sorry for myself, feeling sorry for Hernán. But before I could stop myself, I stuck my arm in the space and swept it. Of course, there was a box there, on the other side, resting on the brackets. Randal hadn't been dreaming. Hernán had lied.

Carefully, I removed the box. It was emblazoned with the blue and red Eveready battery logo, the cat jumping through the 9 in the "Nine Lives" motto. It was heavy, and my balance was shaky as I brought it down. It was taped shut, and I used my car key to cut through the tape. When I opened it, I was astonished. I felt the tears well up in my eyes. The box was filled with more than a dozen grenades and some dozen pistols. It terrified me. In an instant, that fear morphed into panic. Now what?

I did the only rational thing I could think of. I put it back exactly where I found it and went to work.

On the Saturday before his birthday, I placed a soccer ball and some soccer shoes I had bought in an oversized box, wrapped it and gave it to Randal on behalf of his father. He was ecstatic, and the next day, when we took him to visit Hernán, he blubbered his thanks along with apologies for having cheated and peeked at him and Érica hiding his gift. He loved it so much, it was worth the cheating, and on and on.

I couldn't even look at my brother.

Mamá uncharacteristically kept quiet. That evening, she was on edge, and Randal was working on her nerves, kicking the ball throughout the house because the rain had not relented. When it hit against the door to Hernán's boyhood bedroom, the latch clicked open and the ball rolled in there. Randal went to fetch it. Mamá caught him emerging.

"What have I told you?" she barked, grabbing him by the arm. "You do NOT go in there. That is NOT your room."

I was completely surprised. It was not an unfamiliar tone; she had used it plenty with us as children. But I had not heard her scold her grandson yet. I felt bad for him. I went over and reached in to pull the door closed to save him from her anger. She turned on me.

"You, either! Stay out of there!" she screeched and reached in, clicked the doorknob locked and slammed the door shut.

Randal ran off to the living room couch. I followed Mamá into the kitchen.

"Easy, Mamá," I said, not gently. "That was stupid. He was having fun. It was an accident."

"Don't get involved. He knows full well he's not supposed to go into that room. I've been telling him all year to stay out."

Something clicked inside of me. "Mamá, tell me again why Edgar Castillo didn't go into that room."

She sucked her teeth. "Because it's a closet. Because it's all the stuff Hernán left behind when he got married. And your stuff, too. You two left me with a huge mess and just took off."

I didn't argue with her. I knew she was lying. Hernán and I never had stuff, besides our beds and a few outfits of clothing. By the time I left, we both had outgrown toys, and the few that we had, had been given to our younger cousins or neighbors years earlier. When I left, our bedroom resembled barracks: two neatly made beds, a small bookshelf in between them and a closet with some clothes and blankets. Above each of our beds was an identical framed photo of our guardian angel.

I waited all week for an opportunity to peek into Hernán's old room. At my new job, I tried to make a good impression even though I was distracted by the uncomfortable feeling that everything was not as it seemed. By Saturday, I had a plan. I feigned illness all day so that, at night, I could insist that Mamá ask Érica to take her and Randal to visit Hernán without me. It would be one of only two times during that ordeal that I would not spend a Sunday with my brother.

They left early. After I dropped Randal off at Mamá's, I languished on the sofa, playing the part of a sick man. For a whole hour after they had left, I sat there, partly because I was immobilized by an encroaching panic, and partly to ensure that they would not turn back for something they might have forgotten. When I couldn't put it off any longer, I used a bobby pin I had swiped from Mamá's vanity tray to poke open the doorknob lock. There was no light bulb in the overhead, so I opened the curtains a little bit on each side and left the door open for the hallway light to filter in.

There were ten boxes piled into a corner of the room. Hardly the disaster Mamá had described. They weren't old boxes. They had the Eveready logo on them, and their corners were still stiffly angular. Their tops were neatly sealed with a strip of packing tape and either mine or Hernán's name was scribbled in thick black marker. They looked like they had come straight from a factory.

I started with one that was "mine." I carefully peeled the tape, but inevitably tore the cardboard in the process. I continued anyway. Inside there were souvenirs from an unrecognizable childhood: a child's blanket with woodland creatures in happy colors and quite a few modern-looking T-shirts with glossy iron-ons. Despite the moniker on the box, none of it was mine. I carefully lifted the blanket and the shirts so as not to disturb a single fold. Beneath them was a thick canvas wrap that I peeled back. Beneath the canvas were two cold, black, steel rifle barrels, and underneath them, smooth, shiny jet-black butt stocks. Neatly tucked into each of the four corners of the box, as if holding the rifle pieces in place, a grenade was nestled in paper, like fruit at the market.

I was less careful with the next box as I cut into the tape with my keys. This one was supposedly Hernán's. It had a smattering of comic books, more unrecognizable clothing and the same canvas wrapping protecting two disassembled rifles and some grenades. The other boxes were identical, except for the varying souvenirs from no one's childhood. I left four unopened, found some tape and re-taped the bottom boxes, leaving the top ones intact. I didn't need to see more.

When Mamá, Érica and Randal returned later that afternoon, I used the excuse of a rare dry afternoon to take Randal out for a walk, promising to come back for dinner. Érica went to her house.

"You're better?" Mamá said.

"Yes, I guess all I needed was a good rest," I said. "Good as new. We'll be back in a while. Make us something tasty. We'll be hungry!"

I couldn't face her, so I nodded in the direction of the door to Randal, and we left. We walked down the newly built boulevard, down toward the forest-not-yet-forest park, past Érica's family *pulpería* and a few more blocks of new development down until we reached the empty lots that led to the river's edge.

"Papi and I used to come here sometimes," Randal volunteered. "We'd throw rocks in the river."

"You know, before this was all these houses, he and I used to come down here to race leaf boats down the river. We'd walk and grab leaves from plants along the way. Sometimes we'd grab one that was supposed to be beautiful or from someone's garden and some *vieja* or other would yell at us and threaten to tell on us. But they never did, and honestly, some of those were the best leaves for racing!"

But there weren't many plants on those razed fields, just some weedy short stalks defying their fate and pushing up through the gravel. So, we stood on the edge for a little bit, chucking gravel at the flowing water and pretending to aim for fish that we'd identify by bubbles near the surface. We then switched the game to finding bigger and bigger rocks to throw, competing and comparing the plop sounds, noting how satisfying the big ones sounded as they sank immediately.

The riverside was abandoned. Scrub, broken bottles, gravel. Even nostalgia wasn't enough to keep me there too long.

"Sometimes, when we leave the river, Papi takes me by Érica's and buys me an ice cream," he told me. "Can we do that today?"

"Okay, but you have to promise me that you'll eat whatever Abuelita puts in front of you. Okay? Because she'll scold both of us if you say I let you eat ice cream before dinner," I stuck out my hand for him to shake in agreement.

He smiled, a rare big smile for him those days, and shook my hand vigorously. His happiness made him super chatty as we walked.

"I love going to the *pulpería!* Érica always gives me extra. After I finish my ice cream, she'll give me a little bag of Picaritas, if they're not done talking. Or sometimes, if they have a big truck to unload, she lets me mind the shop because I'm good at math, and she, Papi and Mario move the boxes from the truck to the back storage room. And sometimes I ask for a Coca-Cola, and she lets me have that, too."

"Who's Mario?"

"He's a friend of Papi's. I think he's Érica's boyfriend. He comes over a lot, but only at bedtime, so I don't really ever get to hang out with him."

"That's weird that they get their deliveries on Sundays," I noted.

Randal shrugged. "I don't know. Maybe the TV and radio deliveries are only on Sundays," he suggested.

"TVs and radios?"

"Yeah, you should see their back room! Sometimes there are so many TVs and radio boxes piled so high, it looks like they're going to fall over. So Papi said I shouldn't go in there, ever, in case they do fall."

The *pulpería* was closed when we got there. The sign said they didn't open on Sundays.

"We'll get an ice cream tomorrow when I pick you up. We'll eat it before dinner," I said to Randal, winking at him.

If he was disappointed, he didn't show it.

The next day, I called to invite Érica over to discuss Hernán's case. "Érica, who's this Mario who delivers TVs and radios to your store?"

"Hi to you, too," Érica said, handing me a large sweaty cold beer bottle. "Mario who?"

I wasn't feeling patient. "Please don't lie to me. Randal says he's your boyfriend, that you two would sometimes come over here at night," I said. "That he's seen him a bunch of times at the *pulpería* while you all unload boxes."

She waved her hand dismissively. "Oh, that Mario! He's my cousin. He's a traveling salesman for Eveready. He delivers on Sundays so he can stay and chat and have lunch with us, that's all," she said casually.

"Since when does Eveready sell televisions and radios? Come on, don't take me for a fool."

She was quiet for a bit. "Juan, there are some questions you're better off not asking," she said. "Stay out of it."

"No way. I came all this way to help Hernán, and I can't help him if you don't tell me the truth."

"Look, Randal has a good imagination. It was just once. Mario heard about some guy he met on the road who wanted to unload some televisions and radios he may or may not have stolen. It was a good opportunity, so we bought them and re-sold them," she said. "Times are tough, you know. In case you haven't noticed, because you live your life in dollars, the *colón* is tanking. We have bills to pay. Considering everything else that's happened, I just forgot about that."

I didn't feel like asking any more questions. We just talked about Hernán's case and the continual trial delays. Now, the National Assembly was planning hearings on La Familia and the murder of Viviana, Érica said, and that could only mean more delays.

At work on Monday, my boss decided I was up to speed enough with the company to go out on deliveries. Two stops on my first venture: a bookstore in Escazú, followed by a smaller one in Ciudad Colón. It wasn't a complicated route, due west on well-marked roads.

I made it to Escazú easily enough, and the sale was a given, which is why I think my boss handed me the assignment in the first place. En route from there to Ciudad Colón, I got hopelessly lost. It should have been straightforward, but the hills and the badly marked roads made it an ordeal. The hot sun before the rain was blinding me on the ascents and the trucks screaming by on curving narrow roads were spooking my American driving sensibilities. I was getting a headache. I pulled over to decompress at a marked viewpoint along the side of the road, stepped out, placed my hands on my waist and took a deep breath. I really appreciated the view: the San José Valley with its necklace of awesomely green mountains. I stood there for a long five minutes, then turned back to get in the car, the boxes of unsold books lining the back of the wagon catching my eye.

I knew what I had to do.

∾ ∾ ∾

"I'm going to help you," I told Hernán that Sunday.

"You've been an enormous help to me already, Juan, by staying with Randal. He's happy. I can hear that when we talk on the phone. I can never thank you enough. I'll never be able to repay you . . ."

"No," I interrupted. "I'm going to *help* you. Even though I know I shouldn't. I'm going to do it for Randal."

Hernán looked genuinely confused.

"I found his birthday present. Or should I say, presents. Let's include the ones you hid in Mamá's house. I found all of Randal's presents. If anyone else finds them, you'll never get out of here."

My brother's face betrayed nothing, but when he repeated, "Juan, you've done enough. You don't have to," he choked up.

I saw before me my little brother: the quiet kid who used to protest when I poured salt on the slugs ruining Mamá's garden. The guy who would give away the American shirts and shoes his grandfather would send him if some other kid really admired them. The widowed father of Randal, that smart, sensitive boy who would surprise me with his deep thoughts about the world when we lay in his bed staring into the outer space his father had created. He was his father's son.

"Yes, I do," I told him. Then I lowered my voice several more decibels. "But I need to know. What were you doing with them? Why would you put Randal and Mamá in such a situation?"

"Listen, it's complicated. Carlos got involved in some intense things. He really went all in. After his travels to Cuba, his eyes were opened. He wanted to be part of the change. He had helped with the Sandinista effort, but then he went to El Salvador and was moved to do more. He wanted us to work together here, like a revolutionary alternative, where we could support our brothers in arms and in thoughts and change the way the world worked."

"But why were you hiding arms in your house, and in Mamá's?"

"Things got hot earlier this year. He was worried that they might be onto him. I offered to store them temporarily while he worked out a plan to get rid of them. But then he was killed, and then, well, you know what happened next.

"It's true, we were creating a clandestine network in Costa Rica. But we weren't trying to bring the war here. The war is already at our doorstep. Any day now, it will spill over the border. They're massacring the people! The Americans are already not-so-secretly fighting against the Sandinistas. They're giving all their money and might to the dictators in El Salvador.

Not even Romero's assassination last year made them change their minds.

"It's only through solidarity that we win the isthmus back, Juan! Why are people not demanding justice? Why are you not demanding that your country do the right thing? The people are asleep. We were just trying to get people to open their eyes. And sometimes, to do that, you need to make a lot of noise."

I ignored his effort to reel me into a political discussion. It was beside the point, I thought. "Noise like what, Hernán?"

"I'm afraid to tell you because you've mythologized him so much. But the statue of Kennedy in San Pedro . . ."

He winced as he told me and delved right into how it was erected to celebrate Kennedy's visit and his push for the regional Alliance for Progress. Those millions of dollars were spread around the region and just went into the pockets of the Somozas, the fourteen families of El Salvador and the military in Guatemala. All that did was destabilize the region even more.

"We got lucky that we got cheated. The *gringos* gave us less because we didn't have a military. So, they couldn't give us the gift they gave the others: officers to train them in anti-guerrilla tactics. Imagine that! Teaching tyrants how to torture their own people," he said.

"You're getting off topic again. Did you . . . I read that in the paper! Were you the idiots who bombed the statue?"

"Not me, per se. But, yes, the group. We tried. The ones given the job just messed it up. It would have been symbolic."

The rest of what my brother told me that day, and in dribs and drabs during my other Sunday visits that year, shocked me. I absorbed the breadth of his sins like punches to the gut, realizing that no amount of prescribed penance would absolve the sins he committed against his country.

He was not contrite, but he was sad. His retelling was mostly somber. If he ever felt it was weighing too heavily on me, he'd make a joke of it, telling me about madcap blunders or inane discussions. But everything he told, every confession he made, every crime he admitted to me, ended with the same emphatic conclusion, like a prayer: "We are not terrorists."

He'd say, "Idealists, guerrillas, maybe, but not terrorists. That's a terrible word. When they call us terrorists, they give us no way to defend ourselves, to explain."

He recounted how the group of friends went from talk to action. Carlos had grown so militant that he had even done stints fighting alongside the FMLN. Each member used their own talents for the good of the group. With the training Hernán received in the Civil Guard, before the car accident ruined his leg, he was able to teach volunteers how to shoot, how to work with explosives, in anticipation of them volunteering at the front, or in case it was needed at home. At work, he'd gallantly offer customers the full-service convenience—on the house—of driving their new car to their door, to save them the hassle of waiting around for paperwork and tags. But in reality, he'd be making copies of the keys and handing them to his clandestine mates, telling them where the cars would be parked so that they could go and steal them when needed to drive arms and people to Managua or San Salvador, or for some other activity.

Those activities included hijacking delivery trucks and relieving them of their cargo so that the group could fence the goods and keep funding their subversive activities. They also included breaking into Civil Guard garrisons and "stealing back" the guns they knew had been skimmed off the Sandinista donations during that war and selling them to the Salvadorans.

He had, earlier that year, been called on for a very secret activity at the beginning of March to teach some comrades he'd never met before how to plant explosives on a car. He claimed he didn't know what it was for, that he was just following orders when he taught the lesson in car bombs. He was surprised to read in the paper how a van full of US Embassy Marine guards had been blown up in Los Yoses on the 17th of that month. And minutes after that, another car bomb exploded outside the Honduran embassy downtown. He said he didn't want to lie to me. Although he was astounded to hear about it, it was a successful day for the group, and he wasn't mad about that. It had gotten people's attention, for sure. The attack had been carried out by some commandos in the group, fresh from the front. He said he was so relieved to hear no one had died.

I told him, aghast, that I had read that one of the Marines had been severely injured.

"When the people and the future are at stake, sometimes there are casualties," he said somberly. He was shockingly unrepentant.

Hernán conceded that some others in the group may have welcomed even more spectacular acts of violence. For the symbolism, not the loss of life or to instill terror, he clarified. He, himself had only ever wanted to issue wake up calls.

Hernán insisted that Érica was really only a secretary and that she never had participated in any activities. She really believed in the group. Her job, he said, was to organize clandestine meetings. Because no one would ever suspect her or her family, they'd store goods every now and then at her *pulpería*. The fact that she remained the only friend who visited him was proof that they had nothing on her, that she had not done much of anything. They had made sure to keep things very segmented, each cell insular. The ones who did not express the right revolutionary fervor were kept ignorant of actions. It was out of respect for their beliefs, he said, not in any effort to hoodwink them.

Mario, he said, wasn't really her cousin. Or her boyfriend. He was a successful businessman, married, with a family, at Eveready. He was sympathetic to their ideas and would donate generously to the cause. Mario really didn't get involved beyond providing money, except for a few times that he helped them in a pinch to unload stolen goods by lending his truck and boxes. He wasn't the only businessman donor either, Hernán said; there were several, many even, but they always chose to remain anonymous to protect their families and their fortunes. Érica had told him that Mario had vanished from her life; he was not returning any of her calls anymore.

Hernán said that Mamá really, really didn't know what was going on or what was in the boxes. She thought she was doing Carlos a favor. They told her it was some pistols and literature for the war in El Salvador. He wasn't sure if she would have hidden that many weapons of war this time around because he'd never bothered to ask her.

Surprisingly, he told me that Papá had helped his group ferry guns and people a few times from his farm in Pavas, Sarapiquí, to the Nicaraguan border.

The group had thought of naming themselves after a Tico who had died fighting Somoza: Comando Carlos Agüero. However, the wieldy discussions over a name had never been settled, so they decided on "La Familia" as a placeholder while they worked on something more official. Something that described their intent better. It was all rather new, and that name was fitting, because they believed themselves brothers and sisters in thought and arms. The paperwork the Department of Justice had discovered in safehouses had used the placeholder, and the press assumed it to be official.

In the end, it would be the only name they'd ever have. After the scandal of a government official murdering a suspect in cold blood, the round-ups of terrorists, the incarcerations and the media frenzy, La Familia became completely disjointed by the end of July. Its pieces were absorbed into the ether of Costa Rican history, and by summer, no one was even talking about it anymore. Costa Ricans had a very short bandwidth for a ragtag group of bumbling wannabe home-grown terrorists. The nation had accepted the crackdown because of its aversion to Communism. The murder of Viviana, however, was an ugly business, and the nation wanted to forget about it and move on.

Hernán and the members of his chosen family were like black sheep, no longer invited to Sunday dinner. They would languish, untried, forgotten by most, in jail. I didn't have the heart to tell Hernán that no one really cared anymore. The country, and even the press, wanted to put it behind them, pretend that it never had happened. These "family" members were aberrations.

The more I talked with Hernán, the less I could see his group of activists as monsters. I remembered Carlos as a nice, talented guy. I had come to appreciate Érica as an earnest and generous woman. My little brother had always been a deep, gentle soul. My late sister-in-law, even, wore flowers in her hair and spread the gospel of peace and love. My mother was politically vapid but patriotic. I couldn't reconcile the people I knew with the idea that they were bad, that they were terrorists.

So, I set to work immediately to atone for all their sins and crimes, and to save my brother's skin and soul. I lied and told Mamá that Hernán had told me where to deliver the boxes and that I'd be moving them as the weeks went by. She acted nonchalant, not even bringing up the lie that they were boxes of our discarded childhood mementos. She only said, "*Bueno.*" The door to the room was left unlocked.

On the first day of my journey of salvation, I put one box in my car, alongside the boxes of books. I was headed to Ciudad Colón, and the route involved long stretches of curvy mountain roads. At a pullover on the cliff side of the highway, I hastily reached into the Eveready box and grabbed the two rifle barrels. I checked for any cars approaching and, not seeing any, I sloppily threw one, then the other down the mountainside. One tumbled; the other came to a stop after hitting a ledge and was still visible from the edge of the road. I slammed the trunk shut and hightailed it out of there. A few miles up the road, I did the same thing to the butt stocks, this time holding them like javelins and chucking them that way to give them more air and a more extensive descent.

I'd grab a box whenever I had similar routes with isolated stretches, to Cartago or Escazú and even Quepos once. Each time, I'd remove the grenades and put them in a black garbage bag that I stored in Hernán's old bedroom closet, afraid of tossing them over a cliff. By box number five, I had grown semi-comfortable with my task. With each weapon that I tossed, I'd convince myself that I'd erased one more year off my brother's sentence and cleansed him of one more sin. That made it all so much easier.

It was on a trip to La Garita that I was pulled over. When the traffic cop came to my window and asked for my documents, I handed him my Illinois driver's license. I hesitated with the car documents because I feared he might recognize Hernán's name. He looked at the foreign license and at me, somewhat puzzled. I said that I was there on vacation, visiting my mom. He then said I had been driving erratically and wanted to make sure I was not drunk, so he ordered me out of the car, made me walk in a straight line and touch my nose with the tips of my fingers. While I was doing that on the side of the road, he wasn't looking at me but at the cargo in the back of the wagon.

"What's all that?" he asked me.

I could feel my internal organs getting mushy and the sweat forming on my brow.

"I'm not sure. This is my brother's car," I started to say while taking my wallet out of my back pocket and deliberately withdrawing a couple of $20 bills from it. "If everything's all right. . . ."

I moved my hand oh so gingerly, exposing the bills.

"Well, since you're on vacation, I won't give you a ticket for speeding," he said, reaching for the bills. "But you can't drive like that in Costa Rica. You should know that. Be more careful."

We both got back into our cars. He left first, and I lingered a few minutes to catch my breath and calm my nerves. I drove around with the box of rifles in the back for the rest of the day and then dropped them back off at Mamá's before heading home.

Randal and I did our regular *Hola Juventud* viewing that night with bowls of ice cream in front of us. After the fear abated of nearly getting caught and thrown into jail for trafficking stolen arms, I was actually feeling celebratory, like I had been given a second chance.

"Can you hear them? They talk about us. Telling lies. Well, that's no surprise . . ." I sang along to Belinda Carlisle, while Randal sang in gibberish English, bopping up and down on the sofa like he was driving in her car. Her messy, tied-up blond hair recalled road trips with Candy.

I waited for Randal to go to sleep and called Candy. It had been months since I'd talked to her.

"John! Oh my god! I ran into your grandfather some time ago, and he told me that you had gone to Costa Rica and never came back. Did you move there without telling me?"

"No, I came down because Hernán was in trouble."

"Oh no! That sweet thing. What's wrong? Is he sick?"

Although I had not meant to do anything but take comfort in the sound of her voice, I found myself telling her that he was in jail and why he was in jail. I didn't bother her with details that might point to complicity on his part, and I sanitized his participation in La Familia. I chalked it up to hysteria.

"John, I wish you had called me sooner. I would definitely have gone to help, to do what I can," she said. "Listen, let me talk to my boss tomorrow and see if I can't steal away for a week at Thanksgiving. Maybe we can even show little Randal how we do it, with a big ol' turkey and some mashed potatoes. Wouldn't that be fun?"

I offered no resistance. I wanted Candy. I wanted her Americanness near me.

Mamá raised an eyebrow when I told her Candy might be coming.

"Hmmm, ¿para qué?" she said, wryly. "I can tell you from experience that no good comes from retreading the past. Always go forward. Don't get bogged down, Juan."

I decided not to press my luck and I let the rifles sit in Hernán's old room for a bit. I turned my attention to the box of grenades in Randal's ceiling. I started with one, grabbing it during a longer-than-usual lunch break. I slung a bag over my shoulder containing a sandwich and a grenade, jumped in my car and drove to the edge of the lots on the Tiribí. My plan was to pretend to picnic-lunch there, throw rocks into the river and then lob a grenade, plop, and make it disappear. I picked up some gravel, looked around and, seeing no one, threw one rock, then another, then another and then, plop, the grenade. Terrified in the immediate aftermath of my action, I braced for a potential explosion.

"HEY!" I heard from behind me.

Stunned, I turned around to see a security guard. I think I went red in the face, not from embarrassment, but out of guilt. I had been caught in flagrante delicto.

"*¡Pura vida!*" I greeted him, as casually as I could.

"What are you doing here?" he asked gruffly.

I reached into my bag and pulled out my sandwich. "I'm just having a picnic and skipping stones," I said as cheerfully as possible.

With a disapproving glance at the gravel and bits of garbage around me, he told me I could not, in fact, be there.

"This is a private lot, not some playground," he barked, putting his thumbs in his belt and drawing attention to his handgun. "Go to the park, it's three blocks up the road. And there are benches there, too."

I mumbled apologies, returned to my car and went back to work. I had been foiled. It was harder than I would have ever imagined to be a criminal accomplice. It was hard to be my brother's savior.

Stumped, that weekend I asked Hernán what to do.

"Call Papá. He'll know."

It was bizarre for me. My father had been a bit actor in my life, just coming in and out during my childhood. Then after I left for the US, he'd send me the occasional letter and invite me over for a dinner with his new family the few times I visited. Growing up, it had been mostly just the three of us: Mamá, Hernán and I. Later, Hernán fostered an adult relationship with our father. Not only that. Papá, who I always viewed as apolitical as I was, worked for the same cause as Hernán.

Hernán was right. Never one to linger over the phone, Papá told me he'd see me that Saturday afternoon and to "do something about your mother." He also told me to move the box from Randal's ceiling to Hernán's old bedroom before he got there.

"And try not to let the neighbors see you. They're nosy. They might ask questions," he said.

It took me three tries and several years off my life to transfer the box of grenades and pistols from Hernán's house to Mamá's. The first two times, I could swear I was being followed and ended up driving all over San Francisco de dos Ríos, first pulling into the Periféricos supermarket lot and then pulling into one of the several love motels along the main road in an attempt to shake my imaginary tail. The third time, I just bit the bullet, pulled into Mamá's carport and tried hard to look casual as I opened my trunk and pulled out the Eveready box.

"Hola, *guapo!*" hollered my mother's neighbor, Lucía, from her carport adjoining ours. She and Mamá had become fast friends when Lucía had moved in a few years back. Mamá called her the sister she never had. Lucía would call us her adoptive nephews. She was always warm and effusive toward me, often offering me a bit of this or that that she had just cooked. She had been bending behind a plant, gardening. Why had I not waited for the cover of darkness?

"*¿Qué tal, Doña Lucía?*" I said, holding the box as I faced her, trying to look cool, as if I was not holding a failed assault on her country. If she noticed anything amiss, she didn't say anything either. I nodded and let myself in. Mamá didn't say anything either. She just made me lower my cheek so she could kiss me hello and didn't comment when I went to deposit the box in Hernán's room.

I asked her to babysit Randal Saturday afternoon so I could go out until late.

"Oh? Do you have a date? I'll just keep him that night."

I insisted she watch him at Hernán's house. Mamá could not have been that dense. But I think she was relieved, maybe even grateful, that I had taken this into my own hands, and she played dumb for me. She didn't make me explain.

When Papá arrived that afternoon, he was all business. He pulled his muddy orange and white Land Rover into Mamá's carport and gave me a quick, manly hug upon seeing me. He was holding worn jute coffee bags in his hand.

"Let's go," he said.

We reached into each box and removed the barrels and butt stocks and put the pieces into the jute bags, which Papá tied perfunctorily. I winced as he tossed all the grenades into the box with the rifle parts and the pistols.

"Don't be a ninny," he scolded me. "That's not how they work. You have to pull the pin out first."

We grabbed the bag of grenades I had been collecting in the closet, and we marched out. He chucked the lot into the back of his truck, in the hollow at the base of the seats, then loosely covered the bags with the detritus of a farm vehicle's trunk. He wiped his hands. It had taken us less than half an hour, and that included re-stacking the remaining boxes with their kiddie cargo so that they looked untouched.

"You'll follow me in your car, right? I'm getting too old to drive you back on that road at night."

It took us nearly two hours to get to Sarapiquí, and the sun was getting low in the sky. Hernán's little city car maneuvered poorly on the rustic mountain roads, so it was slow going. When we finally arrived, Papá stopped at the edge of his long driveway, got out to open the gate and came over to my car to tell me to leave it there and hop into his. I let him advance, then closed the gate behind him and jumped into the Land Rover. We drove overland, past his house, through some fields and reached the back end of his finca, marked by a rough barbed-wire fence. He put on gloves and pulled back a section of the fence that I saw had already been cut through and told me to hustle, to get the bags and box out of the truck.

Papá had already dug a deep hole on the neighboring property the day before. Not to worry, he said, because it was the neglected far end of a co-op dairy farm, and only the farm dogs ever found their way there.

We put the rifles, the pistols and the grenades in the ground, and then he handed me a shovel that I hadn't seen lying by the fence. After I filled the hole, Papá laid branches and brush over it. Then he called me over to his side of the fence and quickly mended the barbed wire he had cut through.

As we walked to the car, he put his hand on my back.

"Plants will grow over all this by next week," he said. "Forget about this now, Juan. What's done is done. You did the right thing."

He invited me to eat with him and his woman, but I declined, promising to come some other day with Randal. I was desperate to get out of there. We hadn't talked at all, and I didn't want to start. I was bothered by his complicity in Hernán's demise. I was hurt by his matter-of-fact attitude. I was confused by his actions in this serene, beautiful part of the world, where all of a sudden, I realized, I never wanted anything to change. I wanted it to remain the verdant postcard of my youth, the perfect little Switzerland of Central America. A country so small and friendly that everyone jokes we must all be cousins. I wanted the myth to be the reality.

I wanted to get out of this Costa Rica that I didn't recognize.

Papá held me back for a second when he dropped me off at the gate. Taking my shoulder firmly, he said, "I know this was not easy for you, Juan" Then, fumbled in his wallet for a worn, folded piece of paper. "I was a fan of Monseñor Romero. Some of Hernán's friends would get me copies of his sermons sometimes. The priest in this parish, ah, he's not inspiring, so I appreciated those sermons. Anyway . . ."

He handed me the worn little scrap of paper. On it, he had scribbled this, copied from one of Monseñor Romero's sermons: "Social sin is the crystallization . . . of individuals' sins into permanent structures that keep sin in being and makes its force to be felt by the majority of people."

"I always keep that in mind," he said and folded it back up after I read it and carefully returned it to his wallet.

I didn't even understand what it meant. I imagined that it was a comment on my complicity: by hiding the evidence, I had washed away my iniquity and had been cleansed of my individual sin.

༄ ༄ ༄

I was on the road making deliveries in San José. I had been daydreaming about taking Randal back to the US with me and raising him there for a few months. How much would Hernán hate that? Maybe not at all. Maybe it would be a fresh start for Randal and a chance to see American life firsthand. Maybe my brother would want to follow and get out of this political wasteland he had fallen into. "Hernán, too, can become an American," I was thinking when it happened.

The earthquake hit on Tuesday, November 11th, while I was driving. I saw a telephone poll tip and heard the screams of people running out of buildings. When I got home, the tremors kept us awake and put everyone on edge into the next day. Some terrified neighborhood people hauled out tents to sleep in Florestal Park, which, devoid of trees or anything that could topple over onto them, seemed the safest place around.

Randal and I walked over to the park, which was somewhat festive, given that there was a large gathering of neighbors there. I was feeling much lighter in my step, the enormous weight of the arms having been lifted off my back and was, despite the general fear of a possibly bigger quake, inclined to be even jovial and sociable. We headed toward the center of the park but were impeded in our path by a large fissure that had opened in the earth. It was raw and gaping, like the maw of a beast. Teenagers were making a game of jumping over it, girls coyly cheering on the boys, who did it gracefully and mocking the ones who didn't and slid inelegantly into the nearly waist-deep crack. I did a running jump and made it over easily. I tried to encourage Randal to do the same.

"Come on!" I said. "I'll catch you!"

He'd come to the edge, look down and refuse. "No! It's too deep. I don't want to fall into that hole," he wailed.

"It's not a hole, Randal. It's not going to take you to the fiery center of the earth," I teased. I persisted. "C'mon, little man! I made it to the other side already. Don't make me go back."

He just stood his ground, arms crossed, tears forming in his eyes.

"Please, Juan, please come back," he whimpered. "Don't leave me here."

I leapt back over, and we walked the length of the scar, to where the fissure was narrow enough for him to step over easily. Along the way, and throughout the rest of our time in the park, we visited with neighbors. Randal played pickup soccer with some younger boys. Teenagers nearby played volleyball. I heard a group of Nicaraguan families; they stuck to themselves, refugees from the war who had decided to remain in Costa Rica. Érica had told me about them; they were being scapegoated by Ticos, blaming them for petty crimes, rising costs and a declining standard of living.

I even found some other *gringos*, missionaries who were using Costa Rica as a first stop on a five-year Christian journey to some deeper parts of Latin America. They were based in Florestal to get acclimated and to learn Spanish. Costa Rica was considered Latin America-lite. They were thrilled to give their aching jaws a rest from the Spanish workout. We conversed for a long time in English. I realized that, besides my phone conversations of late with Candy, I hadn't spoken much English since I had arrived. I missed the sound of it. It was, truly, my preferred language.

"You're very lucky," one of the missionaries said to me.

Ken had brought his wife and four little kids with him. He confessed that they were falling in love with Costa Rica and that leaving might be hard, even though they knew their calling was elsewhere.

"This is a magnificent country. Your country. It gives us hope for the world," he said.

I lowered my eyes, pursed my lips and nodded slightly. I didn't bother correcting him, telling him I was an American citizen. It always sounded petty to tell people that, actually, I had chosen the United States a long time ago.

About two weeks later, I took Randal with me to pick Candy up from the airport. She was a bright presence right off the plane. Her yellow hair and confident stride turned men's heads as she made her way toward us.

"Look Randal! There's Candy," I said to him, cautiously excited, seeing her coming out of the gate.

We had never become hostile, but the cold, civil distance that had led to our divorce had only begun to really melt in the past weeks, during which we spent a lot of money on long-distance calls that lasted into the night.

"She's pretty. She looks like Barbie," he said, then added excitedly, "Juan! She looks like Kim Carnes!"

Candy was upon us.

"Joooohhhhnnn!" she cooed and embraced me. Then she bent down and said to Randal, "I met you when you were an itty-bitty baby. You are soooo cute!"

Randal didn't understand her, but he had practiced his greeting with me the day before. "Hello, Candy. Nice to meet you." Uncharacteristically for my shy nephew, he gave her a kiss on her cheek.

Candy took him by the hand and gave us a big smile. "We're going to have the best time together."

While we talked non-stop all the way home, Randal played with some action figures in the back seat. Candy was fondly recalling her visit to Costa Rica with me years earlier, when we were still married, and Randal had just been born. She noted development and said she was impressed by the improvement.

Mamá was at Hernán's house to greet us but made some weak excuse as to why she would be unable to spend the day with us. That was fine by me. I wanted Candy to myself for a while, without my mother's visual interference.

It was a pleasant start to her vacation, and we made plans to take her to the volcano on Saturday and maybe to the Atenas area on Sunday after a quick visit to Hernán. That Friday, I told her I'd take her dancing with friends from work, so she could meet them. I was looking forward to the diversion and the distraction.

"You know, John, you look good here," she said, standing in the doorway between the kitchen and living room. "It suits you. So does that mustache. Very, very Latin, if I may say so."

She flashed me a flirty smile, and I chuckled and stood up, unfurling the sheet I had taken out of the closet. "Take my bed, Candy," I said to her. "I'll make up the couch."

"Oh, well, now, there's no need for that, John. We know each other much better than that. We can share the bed. No need you getting a backache from my visit."

With Thanksgiving two days away, Candy decided that we should expand our dinner beyond just the three of us and ordered me to invite more people. So, I told Mamá to come, and she asked if she could bring her neighbor, Lucía, whose brothers, sister and parents had emigrated to the United States and whose husband would likely be sleeping off his drunkenness at that hour. We invited Érica, who also was keen on meeting Candy.

There were no turkeys at the butcher shop, so Candy and I bought two big chickens instead. We prepared mashed potatoes and green beans, and Candy even managed to find marshmallows for the sweet potatoes. Mamá brought *gallo pinto*, Érica brought beer and Lucía brought flan for dessert.

We left *Hola Juventud* on for background music at Randal's request and segued to playing Hernán's albums on the record player when the program ended. Candy insisted on saying grace, and Mamá nodded approvingly. After we prayed, I led the table in a round of *viva siempre el trabajo y la paz* instead of saying "Amen," for old time's sake. Then, we tucked into the meal and dessert, and then more beer and coffee. Candy even tried to explain the Pilgrims and Indians in her pidgin Spanish, which no one understood. Everyone fell into hysterics when she, determined to get the story across, began to pantomime a turkey strutting around the table.

It ended late for a school and work night, and we were all exhausted but happy. When I sent Randal off to bed, Mamá volunteered to tuck him in.

Before he left the table, he said to us all, "That was fun. I wish Papi could have been here."

It was the first thought I had given to Hernán that whole night.

∾ ∾ ∾

Candy and I had been getting along very well that entire week. She was a hit at Cocoloco in the trendy El Pueblo, the high-end shopping center that also housed a couple of popular discotheques. Her *gringaness* stood out on the dance floor and turned heads. If I wasn't right next to her, there was always some random guy or other coming up to offer her a drink or to take her out to dance. She was a hit with my co-workers and their wives and girlfriends, all of them impressed that she would stay on the dance floor beyond the English-language pop music and dance to the Spanish-language music.

"Don't be so surprised," I said to them, laughing at their amazement. "*Gringos* love *merengue*. It's easy to follow, one-two, one-two."

Candy, for her part, enjoyed herself and had only nice things to say about my friends, most of whom could manage high-school-English conversation and were generous with her terrible Spanish.

On our way home, in the wee hours of the morning, she put her head on my shoulder and said, "You know, John, this wouldn't be such a terrible place to live for a while."

Our visit to Hernán that Sunday was short because Candy proved to be too much of a distraction in the room. Her foreignness and English speech garnered too much attention in a way that made us all a bit uncomfortable; it seemed all ears were only on us. Randal, Mamá and Érica were along for the visit, and we had a pleasant enough time, but Hernán and I barely spoke that day. His son filled his ears with little-boy talk.

The women expressed pity for his circumstances. They truly believed Hernán was a prisoner of conscience. Érica kept quiet when the other two opined that it was too bad he had some dumb ideas and some questionable friends, but none of the women believed him to be complicit in any real crimes. Hernán, to them, was a good man who had unfortunately been swept up in a moment of hysteria. Mamá and Candy either didn't know of or had totally dismissed the media accusations against La Familia members. If they had even a moment of criticism for Hernán, it would only have been in agreeing that the crackdown had been necessary to destroy this group and make sure nothing like it ever had another chance to rear its head in Costa Rica again. Beyond our circle, the feeling was widespread: unchecked revolutionary ideas could spread like lice in a classroom and contaminate all the kids. Better to pick them out and crush them the minute you saw them.

Candy's week-and-a-half visit was fruitful for us. We decided we owed it to ourselves to give us another try, and because I was stuck for the foreseeable future in Costa Rica, she decided to move here to live with me. We figured it would be only for another six months or so and that uprooting Randal for an American sojourn maybe wasn't in his best interest, after all. We set her return for after the Christmas holidays.

Randal, who because of Candy had begun to call me "*Yon*," was excited. He liked Candy. He even let her sing along to Bette Davis Eyes.

In the weeks between Thanksgiving and the New Year, I was a newly freed man without a care in the world. I had done my brother's penance and I had reconciled with the love of my life. I immersed myself in work. On weekends, I indulged at El Pueblo. I took Randal skating at Salón de Patines Music on weekends, where the soundtrack mirrored our weekday evening TV. I even booked a "family" vacation in January at Jaco Beach Resort for when Candy returned. I figured it would be a chance for Mamá to warm back up to her, and it would be a great escape for Randal.

Candy had barely time enough to put down her bags before we took off down the so-called highway to Jaco. Once the asphalt ended not far enough outside the San José area, it was slow going, with trucks, bicycles and vendors sharing the rutted road. The 100 km trip took us more than four hours, including our stops for bags of *mamones* and *pejibayes*, locally harvested fruits. We arrived sweaty and dusty and headed straight to the hotel pool after getting settled in our rooms.

It was the good life. I was feeling incredibly happy.

A few nights into our stay, after Randal had gone to bed and Mamá had settled into the room with him, Candy and I went out to the hotel bar, which had a dance floor and a combo playing. As usual, she garnered attention there, a *gringa* dancing *merengue* like she was born to it. A few rounds in, we befriended another couple and migrated over to their table. At some point, in between sets, the women were making efforts at cross-lingual conversation, and the guy and I started talking generalities: my time in Chicago, my return to Costa Rica with my "wife." We agreed to get together in San José, where we both lived. He lived in Rohrmoser, a section of San José way tonier than mine, but my semi-*gringo* status and my blond American wife were social equalizers. I took out a business card, scribbled our phone number on the back and handed it to him. He read it, looked at me and read it more carefully.

"Any relation to Hernán Brenes Madriz?" he asked me, raising an eyebrow.

In my six months in Costa Rica, no one had asked me that question. Not once. Those who knew I was his brother were sympathetic toward his plight, uncaring of his politics. At work, it never came up. I wasn't sure how to answer.

"Hmmm. Why do you ask?"

"Well, you work for this radical left publisher, commies, and you have the same names as one of those *hijueputa* terrorists. So, well," he stammered, then quickly added, with a laugh, "Sorry, my friend. Sorry. I drank too much."

I let the moment stand before finding my courage. "He's my brother," I finally said.

His face transformed into a scowl, and he snapped his fingers to get his wife's attention to leave. She looked stunned but obeyed his command and stood up abruptly. The guy had a look of disgust on his face and made a show of handing me back my business card, like it was contaminated.

"*¡Pendejos!*" he said as he walked away.

"John! What was that about?" Candy asked.

"Just some asshole," I said to her. "He didn't like the cut of my jib, I guess."

Candy wouldn't take her eyes from me. I knew she wouldn't let this lie.

I wasn't wrong. Once we returned to San José, she gave me a few days to catch my breath and get back into the post-holiday swing of the workweek. She settled into her role as "mother" and housewife before bringing it up again.

"Don't lie to me, John. You know we have too much at stake here. Tell me what happened at Jaco with that guy. I know you're hiding something."

"It was not a big deal. He recognized our family names and said I was working for communists. I told him I was Hernán's brother. He was a prick. Don't worry about it."

"You know, your grandfather and I talked about this before I came over. It's a small country. It's not unlike our Louisville. If you're anyone who's anyone, people are going to know you. If you want to get ahead, you need to care about that. Your *abuelito* warned me that it would be hard for you here because people know your name. They'll assume you and Hernán are one and the same."

"Candy, first of all, we're nobodies here. Secondly, Hernán is not a bad guy. I can't say I understand his politics, but I do know that he and his group care about people. My dad said something to me the last time I saw him about how our individual sins lead to social sins, you know, where a whole country ends up doing wrong. I think La Familia was trying to right those wrongs. Sure, they went about it stupidly. But I'm coming around to the idea that I can't begrudge them for at least trying. I can't say I ever gave the things they thought about a second thought, you know."

"Oh my God, John! You're falling for it. Snap out of it. This is commie propaganda, making you think that it's your fault that other people are suffering. You're the one who's not a bad guy. You've never tried to hurt a person in your life." She took my hand and softened her tone. "I know it's been a lot for you, what with Randal and all. And I know you feel badly for him because he's your brother and he's stuck in jail. But maybe jail is the best place for him right now, so he can sit and think about how stupid he was, how stupid those ideas were. I mean, look around you! Costa Rica is wonderful!

Listen, this goes for anywhere, not just here, but if we all just concentrate on Number One, doing what we can to get ourselves ahead, if we each of us focus on working and saving and making ours a better life, then all of society benefits. The good trickles down! That's Civics 101. Think about it, John. Everyone has to be rowing in the same direction or the boat sinks. Your brother's pals, they were messing with the flow. So tell me, what were they really trying to do?"

After all those hours talking with Hernán, and with Érica, I still really didn't know the answer to that question. I couldn't for the life of me grasp what change they actually thought they'd achieve by bombing things and scaring people. No matter how many times he explained it to me, I still thought he was wrong. Acts of violence could not achieve peace anywhere. He'd say he hated to be referred to as a terrorist because La Familia never targeted civilians. The group felt one with the people and took actions only against the government. But he didn't mind being called a guerrilla, a fighter, a David against Goliath. He was so earnest. I couldn't shake the thought that maybe in all their stupidity, they knew something I didn't have the mental capacity to grasp. Or something that I didn't want to think about. I didn't have that fight in me.

I stood up and went to the side of the table where Candy was sitting and put her head against my chest in an embrace.

"You're right, Candy. Abuelito might be right, too. But I'm stuck now. I won't leave Randal. It is what it is."

"No, it is not. We're in this together now, John. Let's make it work. I'm not saying leave Randal. But fix it for yourself. Don't get pulled down in your brother's muck. Maybe you start by finding a new job. If what that guy said about the publisher is true, then you're just putting a target on your back by working there. Pretty soon, everyone will assume you and Hernán are one, and you'll be blackballed."

In the weeks that followed, I gave it some thought. I was spurred on by the headlines, which I had taken to reading in order to share some news with Hernán on my Sunday visits. In the first couple of months of the year, terrorists seemed to be coming out of the woodwork. The son of a prominent Iranian businessman was kidnapped outside of Leonardo's, a discotheque that Candy and I sometimes went to. Then an attempted kidnapping of a Salvadoran businessman had left three dead in Tres Ríos. The police announced that the perpetrators were members of the Central American Revolutionary Workers Party. Then the door of a Nicaraguan counter-revolutionary leader was blown off in Rohrmoser, of all places!

The final straw for me was the discovery of $250,000 worth of arms and ammunition in a private house, which was purported to be one of the biggest pipelines to the guerrillas in El Salvador. That one sent chills up and down my spine and made me start actively looking for a new job. Although I liked my job and my colleagues, I can't say I read much of what I sold: dense books on politics and economics, not really my speed. Nothing about them seemed overtly revolutionary, but, still, I refrained from asking my colleagues about them. I hesitated to know too much about their politics. Instead, I mentioned how I needed a higher paying position now that I had Candy to support again. There were no hard feelings as far as I could tell. My English and accounting background easily helped me land a position at a textile exporting company owned by the uncle of a colleague. My office wished me well, we promised to keep meeting up at El Pueblo on weekends, and I left them, feeling a little guilty that I didn't have the courage to admit to them why I felt the need to move on.

Candy cooked me a celebratory dinner after I called her with the news of the new job. She and Randal even had little party horns that they'd picked up at the *pulpería*, and they feted me with loud toots as I walked through the door.

"Every day begins with new possibilities! To progress and peace," was the toast she gave.

For her part, Candy had connected with the American and Canadian missionaries and, although neither of us was particularly religious, she adored their company and they hers. They let her tag along to their church-sponsored Spanish lessons every day. She was improving, and more importantly, she was making friends.

Randal was improving his English, which Candy insisted upon after school each day. "It's for his own good," she said, noting that his elementary school lessons in English were little more than vocabulary lists. "The future is English. If he doesn't learn to speak it, he'll never get ahead."

I could tell that Hernán didn't entirely agree, but by this point in his incarceration, my brother was feeling trapped. Besides reminding me not to *agringar* his son too much, he repeatedly would ask me to thank Candy for doting on Randal.

∾∾∾

My new job wasn't nearly as sociable as my old one. It was just five of us in the factory office, including the owner, who spent large chunks of the week there, a real hands-on kind of guy. He had studied in the US back in the day and was a fan of all things American. He would often come around and take me to lunch or just sit for coffee and chat in the afternoon.

One day he surprised me by asking, out of the blue, "What's the deal with your brother?"

I wasn't too surprised that he knew who I was. After all, I was recommended by his nephew, a friend of Érica's, and who knows, maybe a member of the same group she had joined. But I didn't say anything like that.

I just said, "He's in jail."

He chortled. "Of course, I know that. I mean, what's the deal with him. Was he or was he not in La Familia?"

I was taken aback. There was no good answer. I just hemmed and hawed, saying nothing and saying everything in my nonresponse.

"I knew the Salvadoran businessman who they tried to kidnap a few weeks ago, a different group they say," he continued. "We were friendly, he was with ADOC, the large shoe manufacturer. We had talked about me and him finding a way to do business together. He was a family man. Business was his deal, not politics. Who knows what world those *pendejos* want! They don't want jobs. They don't want to get ahead. It's envy! Thank God, he's all right. I bet he doesn't come back here any time soon. I've already shelved the idea of us working together, for now. They blew it for me."

I nodded my head but still said nothing. He let me off the hook, but then asked if Hernán's incarceration was the reason I was back in Costa Rica.

"Yes. I came to help Mamá with his son, and now I'm staying with his son in his house . . . even driving his car... just to keep everything normal for little Randal, you know?"

"Well, that's better than what I feared. I took a chance with you because I needed someone. But I thought maybe they kicked you out of the US. That cowboy president of yours is the real thing. *¡Un gran hombre!* He's not taking any shit from the Soviets and he, for sure, isn't going to let them invade us here," he said and casually added, "Are you worried they won't take you back?"

I laughed. I thought he was joking. I told him I had become an American citizen a decade earlier.

"So what? That means nothing. If they think you've become a communist like your brother, they can just stop you from going back, just like that," he said, and snapped his fingers. "If I were you, I'd stay far away from that brother of yours. You were right to leave the university publisher: it's a hotbed of communist sympathizers, like that nephew of mine. They think they know everything, but it's just a phase they're going through. You should have seen my nephew during the elections, all *el pueblo unido jamás será vencido* and idiocies like that. *¡Tonto!* But he'll grow up, and he'll want to start his own business like me, and like his father, and he'll see how the world works and he'll abandon all that. Everyone does. The only ones who stick with it are the lazy ones, the ones who don't want to work for a living, the ones who want those of us who do work hard to give them everything they need. Nah! You can't have it both ways. You can't have wealth *and* socialism. Sometimes we get lost in our own ideas here, pumping more and more money into pensions and social security and state-owned businesses. We'll never get ahead if we keep going down that road.

"Like I said, you were smart leaving that publisher. If I were you, though, I'd make sure Uncle Sam knows that you haven't succumbed to *babosadas*, like your brother. Ha! Or the next thing you know, they'll be raiding your house looking for secret plans and guns and telling you to stay the hell out of the United States forever!"

I hadn't even known that was a possibility! I had thought of my blue passport as my talisman. I told Candy about it.

We both agreed: we needed to do something about it, immediately.

Hernán had said that all of the newspapers in the country were super conservative. I couldn't tell one way or another, but I could report to him that there was wall-to-wall coverage of the violent terrorist events at the start of the year, and the coverage of the newly elected president Luis Alberto Monge often focused on the dire economic crisis he was inheriting and the wars on the isthmus.

"Did you hear that Edén Pastora switched sides?" I reported to Hernán in April. Pastora, known as Comandante Zero, was a nationalized Tico and Sandinista commando who had quit his post as Nicaraguan defense minister the previous year. When Pastora was the Sandinista hero living in northern Costa Rica during the war, the press loved him. Even Figueres' son, Mariano, volunteered to serve with him and his soldiers, training in the supposedly clandestine camps in the north for battle in the war's southern front.

"The newspapers had a field day! He showed up in San José and said he's the real deal, that the Sandinistas had betrayed the revolution," I said.

"No surprise the newspapers loved that! Just like the fanfare around the Sandinista uprising in the 70s. You want to know what one of the best kept open secrets is now? That the *yanquis* are paying for all this repression and violence in El Salvador and with the contras. They're feeding the papers these stories. You better believe the contras are the heroes of the story! They have to be because the *gringos* want it to be that way. And remember what I told you? We dug our own hole by letting the *gringos* float us for so long. So now, Monge has to go along if he wants the money," Hernán said, but he didn't seem as amused by this bit of juicy news I had brought to entertain him. He let that comment hang and got sullen all of a sudden.

"Memory is short, man," he said. "History is not about what could have been. It's about what becomes. History will forget all about us once the winds start blowing in a new direction. I feel the breeze already."

I didn't tell him that I would be delighted if history forgot La Familia and erased Hernán's involvement in it. In fact, in the reports of all the terrorist acts that year so far, La Familia was hardly ever referenced. The blame was not put on revolutionary Ticos anymore but on the Nicas and the Salvadorans and the Soviet communist influence. Even the Argentines would get honorable mentions. The few times I could get my hands on it, *The New York Times* would confound me with dense stories about the Reagan administration's insistence that the Sandinistas were funding the Salvadoran rebels, and both of them were being funded by Cuba and the USSR. That's why it behooved the US to fund the contras in the fight against global communism. It let me believe that Ronald Reagan and his team really gave a shit about what went on in our poor little countries. In short, the few dozen guerrilla neophytes in La Familia had been an abject failure and they had officially been replaced by other bigger, scarier, more competent nemeses.

It also seemed that in the official erasure of the disagreeable recent history of young, wayward Tico revolutionaries bringing violence to the vaunted Switzerland of Central America, my brother's legal case kept falling through the cracks. His trial would be delayed over and over and over again, with no one in a position of power inclined to grease the wheels of justice.

In the meantime, Candy, Randal and I became our own little family. In the absence of her own Costa Rican friends,

Candy would take Randal to play with the children at the houses of the American and Canadian missionaries she had befriended. His English improved by leaps and bounds, so much so that even Mamá was suggesting that we transfer him to the bilingual Lincoln School that the *gringo* children attended. For his own good, of course. Hernán had flinched at the suggestion, so I told the ladies to give it a bit more time so Randal could have some more continuity until his father got out of jail.

Our life was enjoyable, mundane, easy. It wasn't unlike Chicago's Pilsen neighborhood. Here we, even me, were viewed as the acceptable outsiders. The locals were generous with their welcomes, but we tended to gravitate on a day-to-day basis toward the other *gringos*, despite their religiosity, because we felt more natural around them. They were earnest people, good people. Ken and his wife, Vicky. Peter and Kara. Stuart and Tamara. They rarely, if ever, talked politics. Instead, they talked about teaching men to fish. They didn't preach liberation, like my father's beloved Monseñor Oscar Romero but talked about empowering people to live to their highest potential. Mostly, we'd just hang out, sometimes playing board games, listening to music and talking about sports, movies and other generalities.

On weekends, though, Candy and I partied like Ticos. And for that, we leaned heavily on my friends from the publishing company, occasional cousins and sometimes Érica and her friends from the neighborhood.

Even Mamá had come around to forgiving Candy for our previous split. "We all grow up," she said to me one day about Candy. "She's not so frivolous anymore. She's serious now. She's good with Randal."

Indeed, she was good with Randal. Physically, she was the total opposite of his mother, Ingrid, whom Randal, I'm sure, couldn't even remember anymore beyond his father's descriptions of her and her photos. He had quickly abandoned our bachelor routine in favor of hanging out with Candy. They understood each other, even if she couldn't understand other people's Spanish as readily as his, nor the other people's English. He even introduced her to another Japanese cartoon, *Candy Candy*, that she'd indulge him with most days of the week. We still would catch *Mazinger Z* and *Hola Juventud* regularly, but not with the religiosity that we used to, and certainly not with TV dinners. Candy would clear away the supper dishes and bring out Monopoly or Chinese checkers or Life, and sometimes even just a deck of cards and play blackjack. For young Randal, this new normal must have been more real than his fading memory of the time before his father's arrest. I considered that a win. I didn't know if my brother could be saved from a long sentence, but I knew I could make his son happy.

In the privacy of our—Hernán's—living room, after Randal went to sleep, we plotted to put me in the good graces of the Americans again and ensure we could escape this enigmatic country of my birth when we needed to. Even if it meant leaving Randal behind.

∾ ∾ ∾

That winter, another terrorist bomb exploded in San José, this time destroying the Honduran national airline offices. And then, President Monge traveled to the US, which Hernán said, was to grovel for more money. He was probably in a bind, I thought, if the United States was his sugar daddy. We all have to make deals with the devil sometimes, I thought, and if that meant toeing the line and, at least, pretending to be completely anti-Sandinista and pro-contra, and pretending to be against the Salvadoran freedom fighters, well, he had the economy of his entire country to consider.

At Candy's suggestion, I decided not to instigate too much more political drama in my conversations with Hernán. "Let him focus on reality instead," she would remind me before my Sunday visits. "Talk to him about Randal. Tell him what his friend Érica is up to, so that he can see what he's missing. Tell him about our visits to the beach and the discotheques and the mountains, so he can remember how wonderful this country really is."

Only once did she suggest I quote the Bible to him. I guess she had been roped into a study or two with the missionary women she hung out with.

"I heard a good one," she said to me. "Tell him he should make it his ambition to lead a quiet life, to mind his own business and to work with his hands so he will never have to be dependent on anyone, and people will respect him."

She beamed and curtsied dramatically and said with a flourish, "*Thessalonians.*"

I groaned, and she laughed, sprung up and clapped her hands.

"No wait! A better one! This is my favorite! This should get him to think. Ready?" she asked with a big, radiant smile on her face. "Okay. *Proverbs*: 'All hard work brings a profit, but mere talk leads only to poverty.' Ta-da!"

I laughed and dismissed her suggestions. "Hernán and I don't do God. But thanks, anyway. I should take you out more! You're becoming a missionary. We can't have that now, can we?"

Family life suited us. We laughed, we shared and we promised to tell each other everything again. That latter bit might have been a little shaky for me. I hid some truths from her. What I definitely didn't tell her was the following: On a particularly rainy morning in August, as I sat at the breakfast table with my coffee and eggs and my newspaper, I was greeted with the horrifying news that the Rural Guards had found a cache of arms buried on a farm in the northern area of Sarapiquí. The story didn't elaborate on the location, but it quoted them as calling the discovery "the tip of the iceberg."

I struggled mightily to breathe, to act normally. I failed.

"John! Are you okay?"

Candy had been watching me, and she stood up to come by my side. I quickly folded the newspaper and feigned a migraine.

"It's coming on like a train, Candy. Can you please take Randal to school for me?" I asked to get her out of the house. "I think I need to lay down a bit."

"Shoot, I have class this morning! I won't be able to come take care of you," she said.

I insisted that I'd be fine, that I'd have a little lie-down and then probably be right as rain and head off to work a little later. They left and I called my father.

"Was it ours?" I asked him.

He had heard the news, he said. He was pretty sure it wasn't ours because no one had knocked on his door, but word was that they had been driving all around the region in the days leading up to the discovery. He couldn't be 100 percent sure they weren't onto our hidden cache. He asked me to come up that Saturday for lunch with Candy and Randal, using them as a ruse, and he and I would take a drive alone to "catch up" and investigate together.

"Papá! I can't! I'm an American! Do you know what would happen to me if I was caught?"

He said nothing for a long time. Then he cleared his throat and still said nothing.

"Look, maybe we can talk about this at lunch. Maybe there's another way. You said it was on the far end of the neighboring farm. Maybe they'll never link it to you," I said.

"Hernán is my son," was all he said.

I agreed to go visit, despite the overwhelming dread that filled me.

Candy and Randal were excited about the visit. Papá's ranch was way up in the mountains, in a beautiful part of the country. Candy's much improved Spanish and her desire to be pleasant intact, she easily spent the afternoon helping my father's de facto wife—he had never actually divorced my mother—prepare lunch. Randal was happy playing with the latest litter of puppies, still penned up in the kennel with their mother. The rain held off for most of that day.

"Juan, come take a ride with me," Papá said while our wives were still putting the finishing touches on our meal.

They barely noticed us leave. I felt as if I was walking to the gallows. Instead of taking me to the far side of the ranch, Papá drove out and around the rutted country roads. He finally pulled up to the closed fence of Cooperativa X, the dairy farm whose giant tract of land abutted the back end of my father's much smaller property.

"Yesterday morning I heard someone say it was here . . . or maybe the one next door," he said, pointing to an unseen sign way farther down the road. "I didn't want to ask too many questions because I didn't think we should risk it in daylight. I went out last night. It was raining, and it was dark, but it looked all right. It wasn't ours. Just to be sure, I dug down a little in one of the holes. There was just rotten jute and muck stuck to metal, just a big useless, muddy mess. So I covered it back up, as if nothing, and threw some branches on top of it for good measure."

He was staring at his lap as he recounted this. "Don't worry, son. They'll never connect you to any of this. Or me, really," he said, quietly. "*Tranquilo.*"

In a rare show of solidarity early the next month, Mamá and Papá both signed onto the public accusations brought against the government by a group that had named itself "Families of Political Prisoners in Costa Rica." The group said the country not only had tortured jailed terrorists but also had delayed their trials. The government expressed outrage at this accusation, insisting that the trial delays had everything to do with the novelty of political violence in Costa Rica, the country and its systems being unfamiliar with how to process the complex terrorist crimes. Candy and I decided I should keep my name off that document, just in case. We felt relieved that I hadn't signed on when Amnesty International later focused a spotlight on it, picking up the torch and advocating for the prisoners, not only those of La Familia, but also many others who had been rounded up in reaction to the more recent bombings, kidnappings and arms dealing. Some, like my brother and his friends, were Costa Ricans. Many more were Salvadorans and Nicaraguans.

It could be that I wasn't being entirely honest with Candy, as I stated earlier. I was troubled by the trajectory of the country. Reading the paper had become a daily affair for me, even if I didn't share most of it in any significant detail with Hernán anymore. The tanking economy, the inflation, the crisis in Central America, the terrorism were always front and center in the headlines. And steadily creeping into the reports was the US assistance to Costa Rica, with Reagan promising supplies of "non-lethal" security and military training, re-placing the World War II-era weapons our Civil and Rural Guards carried with M-16s, just like those used by the American military, just in case the Nicaraguan soldiers crossed our border. In return, the US kept trying to get Costa Rica to step away from its declared neutrality and to promise to instill more free-market reforms. The US wanted our loyalty, our land to train contras, our hearts and souls. If we were unique, as Érica had insisted months ago, our individuality was quickly being smothered. Money always wins out; we were getting stuck up against a wall, poster children in the US's cold war against communism.

The bedtime stories of our successes—the universal health care, the free education, the equality, the middle class, the democracy—seemed trivial, more like fairytales, compared to global politics. The news about our economy weighed on me now. What would happen if we ran out of money? What would happen to the myth of Costa Rica? I had started to think about that, putting aside all the revolutionary bullshit, maybe Hernán was not wrong: We did need to fight the good fight in defense of our way of life.

But unlike Hernán, I was not a fighter. I longed for a return to ignorance. I wanted not to care. It was easier for me to look out for me and mine. I'd continue to work hard, save, be a decent man, and in return, life would reward me with peace and groceries in my old age. It was every man for himself time. I really did believe this.

At the end of October, Candy came home out-of-breath, carrying a copy of *The Tico Times*. She had been meeting with women from the American Society to plan a Halloween party for the kids.

"John! He's coming. The president is coming! Reagan will be here!" she said, excitedly. "This is your chance."

I laughed. "My chance at what? 'Hi Mr. President. I'm John Brenes. I'm a proud American. Please let me back in!'"

"Be serious," she said, sternly. "Alice at the Society told me that they'll be needing all sorts of help for his visit, planning events around it and such. She said they would need to hire a whole bunch of drivers to take people back and forth, and they'll need people who can speak both English and Spanish. She suggested you apply. John! This is your chance to prove that you're a patriotic American! You can get this job."

It wasn't a crazy idea. Ronald Reagan would be visiting Costa Rica as part of a Latin American tour. It would be the first time an American president had visited since Kennedy. It would be a very big deal. I knew my boss would give me the days off, the visit being in quiet December and he being a huge Reagan fan.

I showed up at the embassy gate in Los Yoses early the next week, my passport in hand. I told the Marine guard what I was up to, and he got on his radio and, after a little back and forth, let me through to the front office. There, I filled out forms in triplicate and answered questions. Why did I want to drive for the President's visit? Because I voted for him, I lied. Because I wanted to make myself useful to my country, I added. Not a lie. The money would be nice, also not a lie. Did I know of any reason why I might not pass a security check? I could not imagine any, I lied. Did I have a valid license? Yes. Did I know my way well around San José and its environs? Yes, I used to be a traveling salesman.

Then I waited . . . for days . . . a couple of weeks. Finally, at the beginning of November, Candy called me at work, ecstatic, to tell me that the embassy had called to say that I got the job. I was to go down there the following day to get my ID card made.

I showed up there bright and early before work and had to wait an hour or more before the right secretary came in to process my ID. I did not mind at all. I had been approved. The United States of America had declared me safe to work for the President's visit. The United States of America had recognized me as worthy to enter its house. One word from the United States of America had healed me.

My picture was taken, and I waited a little longer. Finally, the receptionist called me forward and handed me an envelope. In it were instructions and dates for the training sessions and the actual event on December 3$^{rd}$ and 4$^{th}$. Also, laminated like a prayer card and hanging from a lanyard, was my ID, stating in bold letters, Embassy of the United States of America, San José, Costa Rica, Juan Manuel Brenes Madriz, Presidential Visit, CONTRACTOR.

"Don't lose it!" the receptionist cautioned me like a child. "You will not be allowed even to the training session without it."

"I won't, you can bet on that," I assured her.

There was no way I could tell her that I would never let go of this card, that I would fight to the death if anyone wanted to steal it away from me. This card might just become my golden ticket to the rest of my life. I left before she could see the tears of relief forming in my eyes.

When Ronald Reagan's plane landed on December 3$^{rd}$, night had fallen already. A group of schoolchildren in blue and white uniforms had been standing there for hours, but the excitement when the jet doors opened caused waves in the stands as the children's blue or red pompom berets bopped up and down. Small US and Costa Rican flags waved furiously in the hands of all the spectators. The minute President Reagan appeared, deafening cheers erupted.

The national anthems were played as the American contingency passed through the receiving line of luminaries and children bearing flowers and gifts. Once Reagan got into his car and his entourage in theirs at the far edge of the tarmac, we contract drivers hopped into our seats, ready to ferry them to the Cariari Hotel for an official gathering there.

I was driving four people in my sedan, two embassy support staff and their wives.

"That was some outrageous security!" one said.

"Phew! I'm exhausted from all that. I've never seen anything like it. The security was tight, tight, tight! I'd say it was overkill, but this country has been a little bonkers this year," said the other.

I volunteered that when Kennedy had visited, I climbed a tree downtown, and we were all so close to his parade that we could have tossed flowers into his car, if we had been so inclined.

"Whoa! That's crazy talk. That would never happen now. No siree. The last time we let this guy too close to people, he got shot. We're keeping our eye on him now," said the first man. "The world needs him. We can't afford to let anything happen to him."

The following day, I picked up just the two men, without their wives, at the Embassy, plus a third person, an embassy secretary. We drove in a long, winding motorcade from Los Yoses to the National Theater downtown, where Reagan would be signing an extradition treaty with Monge and making a speech.

Hours later, I picked up my passengers at the front of the theater, and we moved slowly in the procession through downtown, breaking off as we needed to get our people to where they needed to go. My guys were skipping the departure ceremony at the airport and going back to the embassy.

"That was a long one, John," one of them said to me as he slid into the backseat and patted my shoulder heavily.

I handed him a cold bottle of Coca-Cola I had taken out of the cooler I kept in the trunk for them. He thanked me but noted with a wink that a beer would have been better.

"At least he delivers a good speech," he commented.

"What did he say," I asked, genuinely curious.

"Well, for starters, some commie jerk from the National Assembly heckled him," he began.

"Yeah, but he handled it well," said his colleague, who had jumped in beside him.

The secretary must have gone along with someone else to the airport because it was just the two of them.

"What did he say to him? Something like you can heckle me here because it's a free country, but you could never do that in good ol' Russia, now, could you? John, you should have seen it! They gave him a standing ovation for the way he dealt with that asshole."

"What else did he say?" I pressed them.

"Too bad Sandra is not here. She would have been the one taking notes. But let me see, I jotted down some points," said the first guy, taking out a notebook.

"Okay, there was the 'We're all from the New World and we need to protect our democracy,' blah, blah, blah. 'Free elections avert war,' blah blah blah. 'Free markets and anti-communism,' of course, goes without saying. That 'agents of unrest' and 'counterfeit revolutions' are trying to fuck with y'all here, so stay the course, 'reject extremism and the force of arms,' and we got your back." He flipped the pages of his notebook to find the interesting notes. "Oh! And this was a good one! I got this verbatim. This was a doozy! He called for 'the withdrawal of all,' I repeat, 'all foreign military and security advisors and troops from Central America.'"

"Oooooh weeee!" said the second one, loosening his tie. "Someone needs to tell Charlie that he needs to pack his bags tonight. Looks like he's been given the boot!"

They cracked up and laughed for a long while, patting me on the shoulder like I was in on the joke. I chuckled along with them.

When I went to do the required exit paperwork at the embassy two days later, I was perusing the American newspapers in the waiting room and saw a story about the president's trip. Reagan, the story said, had insisted that he didn't come with any plan for the Americas, but just to get to know the views of his counterparts. What genuinely surprised him, he said, was that we were all "individual countries" that he had previously lumped together as simply Latin America.

In the days and weeks after Reagan's visit, the local newspaper editorials stopped short of saying "Long live Ronald Reagan, our lord and savior!" But the sentiment seeped through their glowing assessments of the sentiments of peace and democracy and prosperity he had expressed at the National Theater. On the social pages, birth announcements were littered with news of the arrival of brand-new Ronalds and Reagans, now joining the ranks of Costa Rican Johns and Kennedys born in the 1960s.

❧ ❧ ❧

With the start of the new year, and my identification as a proud American laminated and stored among my important documents, Candy and I casually began exploring the idea of not leaving Costa Rica, of setting down roots here. Knowing I belonged somewhere opened new vistas for me. Our friends were delighted. Ken even told us about a house for sale, a few doors up from him. A *gringo*-Tico family had given living in Costa Rica a go more than a year ago, but the failing economy drove them to Florida in search of a sunnier economic outlook. That family's daughters, he said, had babysat all their kids while they were here. They were popular, but their house, in this depressed market, was languishing unsold.

"You can probably get it cheap at this point," he noted.

We went to see the house. It felt almost new, even though a faint smell of mildew had begun to permeate the unopened spaces. We didn't say no but insisted that we needed to think about it.

When I told Hernán about what we were thinking, about going to see the house that was walking distance from his house and Mamá's house, he was not as ecstatic as I had imagined he'd be. Allowing that it would be "nice," he cautioned me to think hard about it.

"I'm not saying you're not a Tico, Juan, but you have to admit that spending a long time outside the country changes you. You and Candy enjoy the fun parts, but you think like Americans," he said. "You shouldn't view Costa Rica as a permanent vacation, a place where you don't have to think about any of the troubling details of life. You know we're real people here, right? With real ideas and real problems? We're not a playground for political theory or dropouts from reality."

His response peeved me but was not completely off the mark. Despite my deep dive into the daily papers, it was hard not to view the country as less significant than the United States. I didn't think that was a bad thing, either. I mean, did everyone want to have to carry the world on their shoulders like the US had to do? I couldn't imagine so. In some ways, it's easier to be the little guy and let others worry for you, I thought. It did not occur to me that we were pawns in the greater battle the United States was waging against the evil empire. I did take heed, however, of Reagan's words of caution, that we should avoid the temptation of thinking we were "above it all" and just fault both sides equally. If I had to pick, I'd stay on the US team and let them deal with the problem at our border. It was part of a problem bigger than Costa Rica. It would definitely be a bumpy road, but when the dust settled, not letting Soviet communism overrun us would be a good thing. In the interest of liberty, sometimes there had to be casualties.

Although we were still unsure of whether or not we would stay in Costa Rica, once Hernán was released, or not, Candy and I were sure about one thing: we'd sell our house in Chicago. There were too many bad memories there. We needed a fresh start. That was an easy task. Lalo and Juanita, who had been paying their dues and saving their pennies, and who had made themselves very comfortable in our house, decided to buy it from us. Because of that, our decision of where to live was made easier. When Candy and I asked her parents to handle the sale because we were abroad, they took the opportunity to announce to us that they had decided to retire to the Gulf of Mexico within the next year. Their house, in Bonnycastle, was ours for the asking, they said, at a can't-refuse price. So, it was settled. We'd be going back to Louisville. After our time in Costa Rica, we'd give the white picket fence a try and raise a family of our own there.

At times, these plans filled me with guilt, as if I was rejecting Costa Rica again.

"It's not wrong to want to have the American Dream," Candy would say when she'd see the doubt in my face. "It's what the whole world wants. Everyone wants what we already have. Fair or not fair, we're the lucky ones."

I let myself agree with her and opened the cage of nostalgia and allowed myself to venture out the door, ignoring what I felt might be my obligation to my family and history. I chose me, us. I dared again to look beyond the horizon.

That summer was hard for Hernán. Time stood still for him. There was no change in his jailed status. Life, nevertheless, moved on. His son would be entering fifth grade after the summer break. In the life of a child, time flies, and if you're not there, you miss it. Hernán knew he was missing too much.

In defiance of Candy's edict, I tried to engage Hernán in debates, trying to keep him using his brain to think critically and politically so that he wouldn't become a depressed mess. I'd tell him how the fight was developing in El Salvador or how the US involvement in Nicaragua was shaping up. I'd regale him with the stories of President Monge, whose cabinet was bifurcated between the war hawks and the pacifist doves. Monge was playing at Mr. Magoo when it came to armed contra excursions from our country, the price to be paid for critical US aid, given the depth of our economic crisis. He'd half-listen, humoring me. But when I brought him news about how this group trying to kidnap so and so or that group planting a bomb, he'd get angry.

"They're idiots," he said about the terrorists. "They're wasting their lives."

I would be forgiven for thinking that he had repented of his political sins. Maybe in some way he had, but not the way I had fervently hoped for.

The idea of fighting for the rights of the dispossessed, for land rights, for the rights of the workers and the poor, all those things they had been passionate about, would fade fast in light of the global war against communism, he said. That idea would become quaint, when the powers that be framed the discussion in the stark terms of communism (bad) versus democracy (good). It was never black and white, and painting it as such was dishonest, he said.

"I've had a lot of time to think in here, Juan. One of the things that I just can't stop thinking about is that we overestimated the Costa Ricans. I regret that now. We thought they'd be with us, that they would rally to correct the injustices we'd bring to their attention, once we explained to them what was happening, which the newspapers never covered," he said. "We grossly miscalculated, it seems. The idyllic world we dreamed about, the romantic way we talked about reforming the system . . . underlying it all was this belief that the people would appreciate our sacrifice, even giving our lives for those ideas. Carlos, Viviana, the others whose names I don't know . . . their lives were wasted. The people didn't acknowledge what we did. They didn't appreciate our efforts."

His voice dripped bitterness. His eyes were sad.

"What a bunch of fuckin' ingrates the people turned out to be," he continued, angry. "What they don't know, what I can foresee, is that once the idealism is gone, when we've let others dictate the terms of our lives, when it's each man for himself, you'll just have gangs and tribal wars. We won't be brothers and sisters anymore; we'll just be strangers to each other. No one will care because we'll only be fighting for our individual survival."

Costa Rica, he predicted, would no longer be unique. It would be like every other country, like any other country.

∽∽∽

In the beautiful, peaceful world that Candy and I were creating in Hernán's house, a great thing happened that June that focused my attention on the here and now. Candy announced she was pregnant. Everyone was jubilant. Randal referred to the coming baby as his sibling cousin and offered to have the crib in his room. Mamá reminded us that we were living in sin and that we shouldn't bring the baby into our messy lives, so Ken offered to do the honors and re-marry us in his living room. It wasn't the Church, but at least it was something, Mamá conceded.

It was a nice ceremony. Lucía, Mamá's neighbor, made Candy a cream-colored dress with puffy sleeves and a high-waisted belt that concealed her still small, but growing belly. Randal was the ring bearer. The missionary wives and Mamá made canapes and tea sandwiches, and Érica ordered a surprise group of mariachis to serenade us. As a gag, our friends had painted "Just Married" on the rear window of Hernán's blue Datsun and tied tin cans to the back fender to make a racket on our few blocks drive home that evening.

We opted against a second honeymoon and instead took a family weekend at a new beach development in Limón, where we played poolside with Randal and visited the city's pristine beaches that I had never been to before.

That Sunday of our Limón trip was only the second time that I did not visit Hernán during his imprisonment. He was totally understanding the following week and had even carved us a little American eagle in the woodshop as a combination wedding and baby gift. But the best gift of all was the news he shared, with a complicated smile on his face: his attorney had told him that he'd soon have his day in court. We ignored the guards and embraced. I had tears in my eyes. This could be good, but it could also be very, very bad.

On September 3rd, 1983, two years and two months after having been arrested, Hernán and his La Familia finally received their verdict. Of the twelve charges originally pinned on him, only one stuck: illicit association. Not murder. Not treason. It was illicit association in a foolish attempt to topple the bourgeois state. He was sentenced to time served, as were most of his nineteen comrades. The handful who had been caught with weapons received up to fifteen years. Hernán was free to leave the courthouse in our company that day.

His neighbors joined us in welcoming him home that night. We had a subdued affair of cake and beer. Érica was there, and she brought along Mario, whom I finally met. At one point, Mario called Hernán out to the backyard for a private word. I watched from the dining room window as they embraced warmly.

"What was that all about," I asked Hernán, worried that Mario would be roping him into the same old shit again.

"He offered me a job, selling batteries for Eveready as a traveling salesman. I start next week," he said, smiling broadly.

Addressing my worried tone, he nodded his head toward Randal, who was oblivious, sitting alone on the sofa and still trying to crack the code on his Rubik's Cube. "Don't worry, brother. It's over. He's what matters to me now. He's what I will focus on. Randal and me. I'm cured now. It's over, forgotten history, already. From now on, *trabajo y paz,* work and peace."

We clinked our beer bottles, and I turned and lifted mine toward Mario, who was watching us from across the room. He nodded back and, shortly thereafter, left the gathering.

Candy and I had packed our bags and took them to Mamá's after the party. Our flight was scheduled for five days later.

The following morning, at breakfast, I read the news story about the sentencing. The reporter described the intensely high-security scene as unprecedented in the local courts and the sentencing as the most extensive in the country's judicial history. It was the most ink La Familia had gotten in years. It was balanced reporting.

However, in the fat Sunday paper there was a caustic editorial that angered me. I tore the page up and threw it out with the coffee grounds to ensure that Hernán would not lay eyes on it when he and Randal came over for lunch later that day. It said the reaction of some of the accused when the sentences were read was arrogant and defiant, confirming the newspaper's long-held theory that it would be difficult, if not impossible, to redeem this type of criminal back into society.

Hernán had already been redeemed, sitting around a prison for more than two years, allowing his idealism to dissolve drop by drop into a wishy-washy memory. If he had ever even been a terrorist, he certainly wasn't a threat anymore. He may have been lost in the woods, but he was determined to forge a new path, his own path, without camp followers. He would be moving on. It was progress. It was salvation.

∽∽∽

Leaving, for Candy and me, was bittersweet. Mamá, Hernán and Randal drove us to the airport. Érica met us there, and so did some of our friends from the publishing company. Ken and Vicky, Peter and Kara and all their kids were there with balloons. Even my father had driven down in the early hours of the morning to say goodbye and to send a little care package to his father. At that moment, in the waiting hall of the airport, these friends, this family, felt more real than the "real life" we were headed back to. Randal, getting taller and lankier at ten, put one arm around each of our waists and hugged us with all his might.

"We'll see you real soon, we promise. We'll bring the baby to meet you," we told him. We spoke to him in English "Be good. Make us proud."

"¡Adiós!" he said. "I love you, Yon. I love you, Candy."

We'd be returning to the country where our first marriage had ended, in the hopes of starting our second marriage fresh, in a new place. Although we'd known each other for more than a decade, it felt like we were a new couple. We held hands on the plane.

At O'Hare we gathered our bags—my original one had multiplied to five between us—and made our way to passport control. Our connecting flight wouldn't be for a few hours. Candy was processed through perfunctorily. But my agent held me back wordlessly, holding his hand in a halt, looking me up and down and bringing my passport close to his face to better read the stamp. He pursed his lips beneath his bushy blond mustache, and I could see the wrinkles furrowing on his brow, where his hairline had receded far back. Without physically moving a muscle, my mind was laying hands on my Embassy ID card, ready to pull it into action if I needed to prove that I was a patriot.

Finally, he spoke. "Wow," he said, and whistled low and long, glancing at my picture page. "That was some vacation! How long were you there, Juan?"

"John," I corrected. "About two years or so."

I smiled warily. He looked me in the face, intently, thumbing absently through the pages of my passport without looking at them.

In the moments of silence, I clumsily filled in the blanks: "Went on vacation. . . . My brother got sick, so I ended up taking care of his kid. Time flew . . . ."

"How's your brother, now?" the agent asked.

I couldn't decide if he cared or not.

"Great. My brother is back home. Everything is normal again."

Long pause. I could see Candy standing at a distance, impatient in her stance, her hand turned up in a question.

He let me through. "All right, then. Wish we could all be so lucky: two years in paradise," he said, his stamp thumping down on the open page. "Welcome home."

# AUTHOR'S NOTE

On June 12th, 1981, five young self-described guerillas, including Viviana Gallardo Camacho and Carlos Enríquez Solano were involved in a shoot-out with the police that resulted in a province-wide manhunt and subsequent nation-wide investigation and mass arrests of suspected members of the leftist revolutionary group, La Familia. Enríquez Solano died that night; Gallardo Camacho was arrested and later killed in her cell on July 1st by José Manuel Bolaños Quesada, a corporal with the federal police. The three others in the car that night escaped. Of the more than thirty people arrested in the aftermath of the Gallardo Camacho murder, nineteen were held without trial until September 2nd, 1983.

This story includes passages of recorded historical fact, but the characters, places, names and incidents are products of the author's imagination or, if real, were used fictitiously to complement the story.

# ACKNOWLEDGEMENTS

If writing is a solitary sport, publishing a book is a team effort. I owe a debt of gratitude to friends and family who supported me, encouraged me and guided me to the final product, *Litany of Saints*.

To the team at Arte Público Press, especially Nicolás Kanellos for taking a chance on me and letting me win the publishing lottery. A million thanks!

To my beta-readers, Loana Martins, Claudio Rodríguez, Catalina Rodríguez Tapia, Tamar Shapiro and Laura Scalzo, whose enthusiasm propelled me. Thank you for your service.

To Mom, Cato, Rigo and Eli who generously shared their immigration stories with me; to Omar, who filled in the blanks on those who didn't leave; to Mauricio and the Professor (who asked for anonymity) and transported me back to the political world of San José circa 1980s: thank you for sharing your memories with me and for loaning me the details for my stories.

To my biggest sister, Ana Rojas, who listened to my fretting and kvetching and mobilized me to publicize my book. Thank you for bullying me into action.

To my husband, Rick Nogueira and my children, Xavier, Luke and Cecilia, who were sometimes early readers, sometimes cheerleaders, sometimes photographers, sometimes web designers, sometimes therapists, sometimes publicists, sometimes ignored, but always supporters: thank you for seeing me beyond my lifelong role of wife and mother and for urging me to go with it.

To everyone, friends and strangers, who "liked" my posts, encouraged me with applause and helped me get the word out. Writing a book, putting your art out there for the world to see, is like wearing a bikini in middle age: you can't suck it in anymore, and it all just hangs out. Thank you for not laughing.